Reena Ellis

and the

Pink Panda

Problem

A DRAGONS OF THE DIAMOND THRONE NOVELLA

A.C. WILLIAMS

CONTENTS

ondensation dripped off the plastic of Reena's large strawberry milk boba tea and puddled in the crease of her tennis shoes. The printed sheet of paper in her lap had been branded with a big ugly I in harsh red pencil.

I for *Inadmissible*.

It might as well have been an *F* for *Failure*.

I failed the agent exam. Reena drew a shaking breath. *I'll never be a Peregrine agent now.*

Four years of training, studying, and sacrificing—for what? An ugly brown envelope with the angry red *I* scribbled on it? So sorry, you're not cut out for *real* Peregrine work. *Go back to your computer, Analyst Ellis.*

No, the letter didn't say that, not in so many words, but that's what everyone else would say when they heard that she had failed.

"I have to tell Dad," she said to the flowering crabapple tree that spread branches laden with blossoms over her head. "He's going to ask the minute he sees me."

Becoming a Peregrine agent had been her dream since she was old enough to know what it was: an organization for genius kids, partnered with the FBI, working together to track down and capture Phoenix Munroe, the world's most dangerous and infamous assassin.

Reena's dad was an FBI agent, so it just made sense that his genius daughter would join Peregrine. And she had, but as an analyst. A data cruncher. Analysts were the geniuses who did the research so the geniuses who weren't clumsy or socially awkward could track Phoenix Munroe out in the field.

Analysts were okay; agents were the real heroes.

Reena squeezed her fists closed against her knees.

Maybe I'm not cut out to be a hero.

Her cell phone chirped happily from where it lay beside her on the park bench. A text from Mica, her best friend. With trembling fingers, Reena lifted her phone, scowling at the screen.

Did you get in?

Reena glared at the aggressive red *I* on her evaluation paper and set her phone back on the bench, screen facing down as though she could hide from her friend.

She folded the evaluation paper up and put it back in its envelope, staring sadly at the phone. She couldn't tell Mica she'd failed, could she? It would make her so sad, and someone as cheerful as Mica shouldn't ever be sad.

If I can't even tell Mica, how am I going to tell Dad? She bit her lower lip, her stomach flipping. *How am I going to tell Jim?*

Jim Taylor, her Peregrine mentor, had been by her side since she joined the academy four years ago. He'd walked with her through every evaluation, every examination, and every challenge.

Her dad would be upset that she had failed. Jim would be disappointed. And that was so much worse.

"Is that Reena Ellis?"

Reena clutched her purple skirt and caught her breath. *Oh no. Not her. Not now.*

The dry grass behind the park bench crackled and rasped with Mandie Beaumont's footsteps. The long-haired teenager draped graceful arms over the back of the bench as she smirked at Reena.

"I thought I smelled you. Did you forget to put deodorant on again?" She flapped her hand beside her nose.

"Go away, Mandie." Reena hopped off the bench, the ice in her plastic cup rattling.

"Don't forget your phone."

Reena whirled. Too late. Mandie had grabbed her phone and was sliding her fingers over the touch screen.

"Mandie, stop!" Reena reached for it.

Mandie held it too high for Reena to touch, violet eyes sparkling. "Poor Reena. Too short." Mandie lifted her chin and sneered. "How is it possible someone as tiny and useless as you got to be a Peregrine agent?"

Reena gaped at her, wide-eyed. Had she seen the exam results? No, they were in the envelope under her arm. Mandie couldn't know she had failed.

I can't let Mandie find out. She'll tell everyone.

Drawing a deep, calming breath, Reena stopped reaching for

her phone and stared at the older, taller girl. "Mandie, give me back my phone."

"Do you know the magic word, nerd?"

Reena set her drink on the bench and held out her hand. "Please?"

"You're no fun." Mandie smirked and tossed the phone at her. "I tried to guess your security pattern too many times. It's all locked up now. Pity."

Reena tucked the phone in her skirt pocket and took her boba tea from the bench. But Mandie snatched it out of her hand.

"Boba! My favorite. But strawberry isn't as good as taro." Mandie shook it at her.

It's not worth it. Just let her have it. Reena forced a smile. "Well, I need to go home." She turned on her heel and marched toward her scooter, which leaned against one of the crabapple trees.

"What? Are you running away? You're such a loser."

"Just leave me alone." Reena shoved her exam results and her phone into the bag she had strapped onto her scooter's handlebar.

Mandie leaned on the tree trunk and laughed, still rattling the ice in the cup of strawberry milk tea. "Poor little Beanie Baby."

Reena tuned her babbling out and fished her elbow and knee pads out of her backpack. Mandie just wanted to get a rise out of her, to start a fight, like she always did at church.

"It's a pity your ugly little carrot-headed friend isn't here," Mandie kept talking. "At least she always has something funny to say."

Reena strapped on her pink elbow pads, not looking at her. "Don't you have something better to do than bother me?"

"Bothering you is the highlight of my day." She pushed off the tree and walked closer to her, sunlight flashing off her rhinestone-studded Converses. "I was on my way to your house, for your information, and I saw you. So, I took it as a sign."

Scoffing, Reena strapped her kneepads on and kicked up the stand on her scooter, wheeling it around toward the sidewalk. Mandie blocked her, one hand on the handlebar.

"I'm not done talking to you, nerd."

"You talk all the time, Mandie, and you never actually say anything." Reena tried to pull the handlebar out of the older girl's hold.

"Rude."

"Yes, you are. Let go."

"Maybe I was going to ask you for a favor." Mandie showed her teeth.

Reena paused. "A favor?"

The unnatural whiteness of Mandie's bleached teeth seemed almost out of place behind the cherry gloss on her lips. "Yeah. A favor." The smirk returned. "And if you do it, I'd owe you."

Reena's stomach tightened. "What kind of favor?"

Mandie clutched the handlebar and leaned down to look into Reena's face. "You can get into a school's academic records, right? The people at Peregrine teach nerds like you to hack into computers.

Well, I need you to do a little housekeeping for me."

Reena choked. "What?"

"You heard me." Mandie scowled.

"You want me to break into your school's records and—do what? Change your grades?"

"Is that so hard to believe?" Mandie shrugged. "I'm failing Algebra, and I need to pass. So, you just fix that up for me, and I'll owe you one."

Reena gawked at her. Surely Mandie couldn't be serious.

"You don't get to judge me, you little loser." Mandie snarled. "You don't even go to my school, Ellis. It's no skin off your back."

Reena straightened. "No."

"No?"

"I won't help you cheat." Reena tried to pull the handlebar away from her again. "And I should report you to your principal's office just for asking."

Mandie narrowed her eyes. "You're not going to do that."

"Or else what, Mandie? You'll make my life miserable?" Reena rolled her eyes. "You already do that."

"Oh, I haven't even started trying to make you miserable." Mandie tore the lid off the strawberry milk tea and flung it in Reena's face.

Reena yelped and tumbled backward ungracefully on her backside, half on top of the scooter and half on the grass. Strawberry-scented milk tea ran up her nose and down her face, soaking into her shirt and into her braids, dripping in pink rivulets through the parts in her hair.

She sat there, mouth open in surprise.

"Such a loser." Mandie laughed, stepping around her. "Trust me, you're going to change your mind about helping me. I'll make sure everyone who matters knows how lame you are, and it's just a matter of time before all of that gets back to your bosses at Peregrine." Mandie started down the sidewalk. "I'll get you fired, Ellis. Mark my words. You getting into Peregrine was a total fluke, and they'll realize you're a fake sooner or later."

Reena stared after her in silence.

Mandie turned on the sidewalk and grinned at her. "If you change your mind, you know where to find me."

Anger boiled in Reena's chest. "I won't change my mind." Her nostrils flared. "And I *will* tell your principal."

"Go for it." Mandie shrugged. "Your word against mine. Plus, he's dating my mom right now, so good luck with that." She winked and waggled her fingers in farewell as she walked away laughing.

Reena sank into herself, sitting still on the dirty sidewalk long after Mandie had disappeared.

Slowly, trying to ignore the bruise throbbing on the back of her leg from where she'd landed on the scooter tire, Reena stood. The milk tea had left a sticky pink residue over her face, turning her shirt and skirt stiff as it dried.

And her hair.

Reena touched the mass of braids her mom had just put in earlier that week, now all sticky with the remnants of strawberry milk tea. They'd have to be redone.

Another reason for Mom to be upset.

Reena lifted her scooter off the ground and unlatched the helmet from where it hung on the handlebar. Settling the helmet over her sticky braids made her shiver, but the last thing she needed was to get caught riding her electric scooter without wearing it.

Reena got the scooter moving homeward, the milk tea continuing to dry on her face and clothes.

How can I stop Mandie from messing with me all the time? Reena gripped the bright pink rubber handles on the handlebar. *I mean, she's bigger and older and stronger, but I can stand up to her. Can't I? I'm strong.*

She guided the scooter around a crack in the concrete and yelped as her helmet smacked the branch of a passing Bradford pear tree. She wobbled and came to a stop, trying to shake the nasty-smelling petals out of her braids. But her braids were so sticky with milk tea, the petals were glued on.

Reena sighed. "Sure. I'm a real tough gal."

She walked the rest of the way to the intersection and used the crosswalk as soon as the light indicated it was clear.

Face it, Ellis, you aren't a fighter.

As she walked, Reena glanced at the still-healing gash on her left arm, a remnant from the literal life-or-death battle she'd been in a few weeks ago. Deep and jagged, it would leave a scar, a memory of how she hadn't been able to defend herself.

Not even a month ago, a science experiment she and Jim Taylor had designed together went wrong—really wrong. The experiment opened a doorway to another world and dragged them and Jim's older sister Barb into another dimension. Andaria, a world full of talking fox people and horrifying Centaurs and strange alien creatures that tried to eat them. They'd barely escaped with their lives.

I wouldn't be alive if Jim and Barb hadn't protected me. Her lower lip trembled. *They're the strong ones. Not me. Just like everyone else in my family.*

Her dad, the marine turned FBI special agent. Her brother, Tay, a marine currently stationed in Afghanistan. Her mom's dad had been a marine too, and even her mom had trained as a combat nurse in the Air Force Reserves. Cecelia, Reena's sister, wasn't in the military, but she was a star athlete, destined for the Olympics.

All of them had shown the world what their family could do. They were heroes, fighters, warriors, winners. What could Reena offer compared to that? How could she live up to their legacy if she couldn't even protect herself against a cup of strawberry milk tea?

"I have to get stronger." Reena stepped back onto her scooter on the other side of the intersection and pushed off again. "I have to *be* stronger."

Swallowing the sadness rising inside her, she took the corner on Rutan street and glided up to the driveway of their house. Using the remote she'd attached to her wrist guards, she opened the garage door and loaded her scooter into the crate she'd built for it. Then, she shouldered her backpack and stomped up the stairs into the house.

Neither of her parents' cars were in the garage.

Maybe she could stave off the inevitable confrontation a bit longer. Maybe she could get her hair clean before anyone found out. If she didn't have to involve her parents in the situation with Mandie, it might be easier.

She pushed the door open and peered inside. The kitchen seemed empty. Even Hermes, the family's giant German Shepherd, wasn't in sight.

At least no one would be there to witness her strawberry-scented walk of shame.

She peeled the helmet off as she walked into the kitchen, wincing at how her braids stuck to its lining. Reena strained her ears for voices in the house and heard none.

Good.

She paused in the dining room and glanced at the far wall, covered in photographs of smiling faces. One photo at the center of the wall stared at her with dark, somber eyes.

Hani Ellis. Her father's older sister, or Eedo Hani as they'd always called her, had died before Reena was born. Brave and strong, Hani risked her life to bring their family from Somalia to America.

She'd been fearless.

She wouldn't have been defeated by a cup of bubble tea.

Reena scoffed and stomped toward the hallway half-bathroom to assess the damage.

The slender, short girl in the mirror staring back at her was a wreck.

It was worse than she'd expected. Her braids looked like she'd been rolling around in the dirt. It had taken hours—hours and hours—to get them done. How was she going to explain this? How was she going to fix this on her own?

"Whoa."

Reena whirled toward the voice. "Cece?"

"Reena, what happened to you?" Her older sister Cecelia stared at her with wide eyes.

"Why are you here?" Reena wailed.

"I live here. Did you get hit by a bus?" Cecelia picked up one of Reena's braids and made a disgusted face. "Why do you smell like fake strawberries?"

"Just stop, Cece."

"We just did wash day. What have you been doing with yourself?"

Reena deflated. Hot tears welled in her eyes, but she refused to look at her sister. What could she say? A girl from school pushed her around and dunked her hair in boba tea? How lame was that?

Cecelia took her helmet away and set it on the toilet lid. "ReeRee?"

"Don't call me that."

"I'll call you what I want." Cecelia took a knee in front of her and gazed up into her face. "Spill."

Cecelia. With her perfect skin and her shiny, beautiful hair and her long legs.

An angry tear escaped one of Reena's eyes, and she sniffled miserably. "I was at the park. And a girl I know was picking on me."

"What girl?" Cecelia's expression darkened.

"It doesn't matter."

"Maybe it matters to me."

Reena looked away. "She threw my boba tea at me."

Cecelia took one of Reena's sticky braids and sniffed it. "Yeah, that's what I'm smelling." She sighed and stood up, taking Reena's hand. "Come with me."

"Where?"

"Just come with me."

Cecelia pulled her out of the hall bathroom and up the stairs to the second floor. They paused at Reena's bedroom where Cecelia tossed Reena's backpack on the floor.

Cecelia guided her into the upstairs bathroom and sat her on the toilet seat while she started running water in the bathtub.

"We already did wash day," Reena murmured.

"Well, I guess we need to do it again." Cecelia dug through the cabinet and pulled out the clear plastic bin where Reena kept her haircare supplies. "Start clipping."

Reena blinked at her. "You're going to help?"

Cecelia offered her a lop-sided smile. "Well, you stink. So yeah."

Dashing the tears off her face, Reena went to work clipping the elastics that bound her braids at the ends. Cecelia did the same with the ones she couldn't reach. Together they unbound her hair.

Mandie would never understand what it took to keep Reena's hair in decent order. Since it was so thick and coily, she only washed it once or twice a month. Mandie had perfect, easy hair. Mandie probably had perfect, easy everything.

As Reena unbraided her hair, Cecelia set out detanglers and combs and moisturizing oil and conditioners and misting spray bottles full of more detanglers.

Reena let her sister bend her over the bathtub while she used the shower sprayer to start soaking Reena's thick, tight curls.

"We won't get done before Mom gets home," Reena said, barely loud enough to be heard over the running water.

"Don't worry about that. You just sit still and let me do this."

"Okay," Reena whispered.

"Why'd this kid attack you with bubble tea?"

"She wanted me to change some grades for her."

Cecelia snorted. "Oh that's real smart. Ask a living moral compass to break the rules."

"I said no."

"Of course, you said no. And then she baptized you with fake strawberry sugar tea."

"Pretty much."

"Who was it?"

"I'm not going to tell you."

"Why not?"

"Because you'll attack her." Reena rolled her eyes. "And that won't actually help anything."

"Spoilsport."

They fell silent as the strawberry milk tea washed out of Reena's hair, unable to stand up against the onslaught of shampoo and conditioner and detangler and more conditioner and moisturizers and even more conditioner.

"What else?" Cecelia asked as she kept working on Reena's hair.

Reena bit her lip. "Why does there have to be something else?"

"I've known you your whole life. Give me some credit." Cecelia massaged leave-in conditioner in Reena's hair. "You and the Russian chick have a fight?"

"The Russian chick has a name, Cece." Reena smiled to herself as Cecelia attacked her hair with a detangling comb. "Mica. Remember?"

"She's from Russia, and she's a chick. Answer the question."

Reena sighed. "No, we didn't fight."

For a moment, the only sound was the detangling comb scraping through Reena's thick hair.

"I—got my agent exam results."

Cecelia went still. "Oh." She let the comb rest for a moment. "I see."

"I didn't make it." Reena's voice trembled.

Cecelia set a hand on Reena's back gently. "I'm sorry, Reena. I know what that meant to you."

Another tear escaped, which Reena dashed away irritably. "I just wasn't good enough."

Cecelia grunted quietly and worked another handful of conditioner into Reena's thick hair. "I doubt that."

"Mom and Dad are going to be angry."

"At you?"

"Yeah."

"No way." Cecelia laughed. "They know you did your best. If you didn't get in? Well, it just wasn't supposed to be."

"Maybe."

"You can always take it again, can't you?" Cecelia frowned. "I mean, you're barely fourteen, ReeRee. You've got a good future ahead of you, even if you don't get to be an agent or whatever."

Her lower lip trembled. "But I want to be an agent."

"Why?"

Reena sniffled. "I want to make a difference, Cece. Like Dad and Tay and Jim. They help people."

"And you aren't helping people now? Just the way you are?"

"I want to be strong, Cece." Reena looked down at her hands.

Cecelia stopped combing and sat on the bathroom floor, gazing up into Reena's face. "You just need to learn that there are different kinds of strength." Cecelia patted her knee. "You got plenty of strength where it counts. Leave some for the rest of us mere mortals."

Reena smiled back at her. "Thanks, Cece."

"Don't mention it." Cecelia grinned. "And you're going to tell me who it was."

"No, I'm not."

The garage door banged downstairs.

"Sounds like Mom's home," Cecelia said. "Twist that mess up and let it rest. We'll braid it after dinner."

"Yeah, I can get it. Thanks."

"Do you want me to tell her?" Cecelia dried her hands.

Reena hesitated.

"You have to tell them, Reena."

"I know." She swallowed. "Yes, I'll tell them at dinner."

Cecelia scowled at her. "Over my birthday dinner?"

Reena blinked. "Oh. Right. That's today."

"You bet it is." Cecelia set her hands on her hips. "And you owe me big time, ReeRee. You got me washing nasty fake strawberry gunk out of your braids on my birthday?"

Reena shrugged. "Well, you only turn sixteen once."

Cecelia thumped her on the forehead. "Go change. You still stink."

"You stink worse than me."

Cecelia stuck her tongue out and twirled into the hallway, disappearing down the stairs to greet their mother.

Reena put all her supplies back into the plastic bin and set it back in the cabinet. She had enough stuff in her room to put her hair in loose twists until after the evening meal.

As she walked toward her room, the scents of cumin and coriander and cardamom began to fill the house from the kitchen. For her sixteenth birthday meal, Cecelia had requested her favorite Somalian meal, beef *suqaar* and *canjeero*, beef and vegetables with sourdough pancakes.

A soft thunk sounded down the hall.

Reena paused in her bedroom doorway and turned in place. "Hermes?"

The giant German Shepherd didn't appear, so it wasn't him bouncing around like a goofball.

Hair wild around her head, Reena wandered down the hall to the door of her father's home office. The lights were off, his computer screens asleep, and all his files were neatly organized on his desk.

But the decorative geode he kept on display had rolled off the desk and onto the floor. About the size of a gallon of milk, the geode was shaped like an egg and covered in rock-like scales.

Tay and Cece and she had a running bet on when their father would crack it open, as well as what color the crystals inside would be. So far, their dad had yet to open the geode.

Maybe someday.

Loud conversation downstairs announced that her father had arrived home as well. Quickly, Reena picked up the geode, as always astonished by how little it weighed. She started to set it on the desk, but she stopped.

A pulse throbbed in her hands, as though she could feel her heart beating in her fingertips.

"Weird."

The rough texture of the geode felt warm too, as though the rock was generating its own heat.

"Very weird." She set it on the desk again, patting it gently. "Stay put, okay?"

She backed out of the office, hurrying to her room to finish taming her hair. Hard conversations awaited her at the dinner table, but hopefully Cecelia was right. There would be other opportunities to apply for agent status again, and maybe she would succeed the next time.

She could still be a hero one day.

Reena yawned and stretched her arms out over her head, and she giggled as her mom thumped the nape of her neck.

"Stop squirming." Ellie Ellis gathered up one of the last sections of Reena's loose hair and made quick work of a long, tight braid. "Now if that ugly girl comes at you again, you send her to talk to me."

Reena winced as her mom pulled particularly hard. "Mandie isn't ugly, Mom. She does modeling on the weekends."

"She's ugly inside, and that's all that matters."

Reena rolled her eyes.

"Don't roll your eyes at me. Repeat what I just said."

"Mandie's ugly inside, and that's all that matters." Reena sighed.

"Good girl."

Hermes thumped his gigantic tail in agreement from where he curled up at Reena's bare feet. The huge German Shepherd weighed more than Reena did.

With a graceful chorus of thumps, Cecelia danced down the stairs and bowed, glitter and sparkles shining in the tiara perched in the midst of her shiny curls. She wore dark jeans, a Coldplay t-shirt, and a calf-length duster.

"How do I look?" She winked at her mom and sister.

"So cool." Reena rested her chin on her fist and grimaced as her mom pulled her hair again.

"The people at the restaurant are going to wonder why you're wearing a crown, Cece." Ellie chuckled with genuine warmth in her voice. "I don't think the Amish do tiaras."

"It's my birthday, Mama. I can wear a crown if I want."

Hermes lifted his head and rolled over to sniff at Cecelia's feet, and she knelt to scratch his big old head.

"There you go." Ellie patted Reena's shoulders. "All done." She pulled Reena back toward her between her knees and kissed the top of her head. "And I'm serious, child. If that ugly girl—"

"I know, Mom. I'll send her to the hospital to talk to you."

Ellie nodded, and Reena scrambled to her feet to allow Cecelia to bend down to couch level so their mom could embrace her.

"My beautiful girl." Ellie hugged her. "How can you be sixteen?" Ellie released her and stood up, gathering up Reena's remaining hair supplies.

"I'll take care of that, Mom." Reena took them from her. "You'll be late for your shift."

The stairwell creaked again, and Reena's dad appeared around the corner of the hallway, thumbing through the cards in his wallet.

Ellie tutted disappointedly. "Jasper Ellis, what are you wearing?" She turned to him and straightened the color of his dark rose colored polo shirt.

He slapped her hands playfully. "My favorite color. Stop fussing, woman." He kissed her quickly and turned his eyes to Cecelia. "Get your shoes on, girl. We need to go."

Cecelia snatched her boots off the shoe rack and started zipping them up past her ankles.

Jasper folded Reena into a tight hug, and she let herself stay there for a moment. Her dad didn't talk very much, but his actions always communicated more than his words could.

Reena didn't know how he could say how sorry he was and how proud of her he was and how righteously indignant he was all in a simple hug, but that was her dad. Maybe it was a gift.

She tilted her head up to him. "What pie are you getting?"

He flashed a bright smile. "Depends on what they have left. Because by the time your sister finishes primping, all the pie will have gone."

He squeezed her shoulders and released her.

"Dad!" Cecelia whined. "You're so dramatic."

"You have not seen dramatic yet." He flapped his hand at her. "We have an hour to drive. Go get in the car. Or all the old farmers will have eaten your birthday pie."

Cecelia turned in a circle, frowning suddenly. "Oh, I need my purse. My ID is in my bag."

Jasper groaned and muttered something in Somali. "The

people are eating your pie, child."

Cecelia laughed and ran back up the stairs.

Reena smiled up at his grinning face. "I'm glad you're not upset, Dad."

His grin faltered a little, and he tapped her chin with his finger. A strange expression crossed his face, tightening his eyes, pulling at the corners of his mouth.

"You are very gifted, Sareena." His tone was soft. "And you have done wonderful work for Peregrine as an analyst. Both Jim and I feel like this was a good outcome for you."

"You talked to Jim?" Reena stiffened.

"Yes, he was already aware of your results. He called me yesterday."

Reena's stomach flipped. "Was he upset?"

"No, Reena. Not at all." Jasper patted her shoulder. "You should talk to him, but you are—precisely where you need to me." He cupped her face in his hands and kissed her forehead. "You are still so young. Your future has not been decided by this one exam."

"I know," she whispered.

He was right. It didn't feel right, but maybe someday it would.

Cecelia came bounding down the stairs again, and Jasper flapped his arms. "Finally. Where was your bag? In the bottom of your messy closet?"

"Ha ha."

Cecelia rushed out to the garage. Jasper kissed Ellie quickly and followed her. They both waved as he backed out of the garage. They would arrive in Yoder just before the lunch rush.

It had become a tradition years earlier that for every birthday, Jasper would take them to a local Amish restaurant an hour northwest of Wichita for a free birthday meal.

Reena hovered in the door until her mom brushed past her with a kiss, headed to her own car. "I'm on a ten-hour shift today, so you'll need to get dinner ready."

"I will, Mom. Thanks. For my hair."

Ellie stopped beside her car and walked back up the stairs to hug Reena tightly.

"I know you're sad and disappointed, but your father and I are very proud of you. I hope you are proud of yourself, Sareena." Ellie squeezed her. "You're a good girl."

"Love you," Reena whispered.

Ellie regarded her for a moment. "I think you should go have lunch with Mica today."

Reena brightened. "Really?"

"Really."

"That's a good idea."

"Of course, it's a good idea." Ellie bopped her nose. "I'm your mother. All my ideas are good ideas."

Her mom backed away and got into her car with a wave. As she backed out of the garage and drove off, Reena shut the garage door.

Lunch with Mica sounded like just what she needed to cheer

herself up. Mica Sherman had been her closest friend for years. She had finally texted Mica last night to tell her about failing the exam, and like the friend she was, Mica declared Peregrine to be idiots.

Friends like Mica were priceless.

She gathered up the scattered hair supplies her mother had needed to finish the disaster that was Reena's hair that morning. Yawning again, Reena walked up the stairs to the hallway bathroom where she deposited the conditioners and moisturizers and detanglers where they belonged, and she replaced the combs and elastics and brushes in their respective cups.

Once everything was in order, she hurried to her room and switched on her laptop with the video call function she'd programmed. She'd built the video call system from two old computers, some faulty webcams, and several throwaway hard drives she'd scavenged.

The video call software pinged Mica's computer, but she didn't answer. So it rerouted to her cell phone. She didn't answer that either.

But, moments later, the computer screen flashed with a text message.

The Fox has me on shift today. You okay?

Reena held down the "talk" button on the keyboard. "I'm fine. I thought maybe we could do lunch."

The screen went blank for a moment before it flashed again with Mica's reply.

I get off at one. Sushi here? Or ramen somewhere else?

Reena grinned. "Sushi there, definitely."

Mica responded with a thumbs-up emoji.

She worked part time at Senjumin downtown. Owned and operated by Jasper Ellis's best friend, Ezekiel Blackfox, Senjumin had been called the best sushi restaurant in Wichita.

The irony of having an excellent sushi restaurant in a landlocked state like Kansas wasn't lost on anyone.

Reena pulled a purple skirt and top out of her closet and bundled some of her braids into pom-poms on top of her head. As she dressed, the same thump she'd heard before sounded outside her door.

Stepping into her shoes but leaving the laces untied, she poked her head into the hallway and listened.

"Hermes?"

The giant dog didn't appear. But the last she'd seen him, he was sleeping lazily on the living room floor.

Reena shuffled out of her room, eyes trained on the open door of her father's office. As she peeked inside, she scowled at the geode on the floor again.

"What?" Groaning softly, she picked up the rock. "Oh no." A large section of the stone flaked away under her hands, revealing a large crack up the side.

Had it broken last night, and she just hadn't noticed? The skin of the rock still felt warm under her fingers, pulsing as though it was alive.

The rock shuddered.

Reena went stiff. Had the rock just moved? Surely she'd imagined that. The rock shuddered again, and the crack deepened.

"Oh no."

Had she broken it? By picking it up, had she made it worse?

The rock shook in her hands, growing warmer and warmer, the cracks spreading across its skin like a spiderweb, peeling away to reveal a throbbing pink light under layers of ancient stone.

Chunks of rock dropped off it, falling to the office floor, and a small furry arm thrust into the air. Reena gaped at it.

It's not breaking. Her heart skipped. *It's hatching.*

She clutched the bottom of the rock—er, the egg—and held it away from her as pieces continued to fall to the floor. Finally, the top piece broke off, and a round face covered in pink fur emerged from the egg.

Reena stared at the creature unfolding from the egg.

"A red panda?" she gasped. "Or a pink panda? A pink red panda?"

What was happening? Red pandas were mammals. Mammals didn't hatch from eggs. And there was no such thing as a pink panda, and there were no examples in zoology of a red panda that was obviously pink.

The creature, still half in the egg, blinked up at her, a startled and confused expression on its furry face. Its gaze shifted to look around the office, its dark eyes growing wider and wider with every moment. The fur on its neck and arms began to bristle.

It opened its snout and snarled at her, and it gathered itself inside the egg.

"Wait—wait!"

The panda leaped out of the egg fragment and hit Jasper's office chair sideways, the impact sending the chair spinning with the panda clinging to it for dear life.

When it finally slowed, the panda looked less angry and more dizzy.

"Okay," Reena said quietly, setting the egg down and approaching the panda with upraised hands. "This is a problem. A really weird problem."

The pink-red panda glanced back at her, little white eyebrows furrowing.

Reena's stomach flipped. *Did it understand me?*

She started to speak again, but a deep-throated growl interrupted her. Reena looked over her shoulder.

"Oh no."

Hermes stood in the office door. The giant German Shepherd locked on to the red panda instantly, hackles rising, hair along his spine bristling. The red panda had the same response, tail turning into a bottle brush, mouth open in a snarl as it reared up on its hind legs.

"Hermes!" Reena stepped in between the dog and the panda. "No! Go back downstairs!"

That wasn't going to work. When Hermes looked like that only her dad could calm him down.

Behind her, the panda hissed and snarled. In front of her,

Hermes had begun to growl, the terrifying thunderous warning he only used for UPS delivery guys and trick-or-treaters.

Reena took a step toward the massive dog. If he charged, she would have to dodge. Getting between him and whatever he was trying to catch wouldn't end well for her.

"Hermes," she pitched her voice lower than normal, "come on, buddy. You don't care about that silly red panda."

Hermes growled more.

"It's all furry," Reena took another step. "You don't want to eat it. Remember when you ate Cecelia's mattress? It made you super sick. You eat this panda, and you'll be coughing up pink furballs for a week!"

Hermes growled.

The panda grunted and squeaked.

"Hermes, let's go find Mr. Bear." Reena took another step toward him. "Don't you want Mr. Bear? Mr. Bear is much more fun than—"

Hermes lunged for the red panda, and Reena dove to the side. The panda leaped off the desk and hit the floor, squeaking and grunting and scrambling on the wooden floors. Hermes stumbled on the office carpet and turned sharply to chase.

"Hermes, no! Stop!"

Reena clambered to her feet and raced after them. The giant dog snapped at the panda's tail as it scurried under the dining room table, and Hermes turned chairs over trying to reach it.

"You guys are making a mess!"

The panda launched off the floor and hit the back of the sofa in the living room, crawling over the cushions and diving into the pillows. Hermes followed, landing with a heavy thump on the couch that sent the much-smaller panda sailing as though the cushions had been a trampoline.

It squeaked and hollered and flailed as it flew through the air and landed in a ball on the kitchen tile.

"Hermes! No! Stay!"

Hermes didn't stay.

But the panda spotted the dog door.

"No, no, no, no!"

The panda bolted out the dog door, and Reena was on its heels. Snapping the door lock in place before Hermes could get there. Hermes slid to a halt and smashed into the wall, barking and scratching frantically.

"No!" Reena shouted at him. "You are in so much trouble!" She spun in a circle and ran to the window over the sink to peer into the backyard.

The panda trotted along the top of the fence.

"No!" Reena threw her hands in the air. "You're in trouble too! You can't leave!"

She snatched her bag from the table and darted for the garage, leaving Hermes to keep barking at the shut door. She strapped her helmet and elbow pads on as she seized her scooter.

The panda was already nearly out of sight by the time she made it outside.

This was madness. Her dad's geode hatched into a pink red panda? Had her dad known that's what it was? Sure, he worked for the FBI, but that didn't mean he knew everything.

I can't let it get away. What if it's dangerous?

It was cute and cuddly, but what if that was just an act? With her luck lately, she'd just released an evil alien that would try to conquer the world somehow.

Number one priority: Get the pink red panda back!

She grabbed the metal case on the back wheel of her scooter and activated the high-performance electronics inside. She hadn't really tested her electric scooter engine on the city streets, but there was no time like the present.

When the lights turned green, she cranked the throttle on the handlebar. The scooter shot forward. Reena kept her feet planted on the scooter and strained her eyes for the fleeing animal out in front of her.

There!

It was still hopping from fence to fence as it went north. Reena bent over the handlebar and focused on the little creature as it loped away from her.

Her scooter couldn't go as fast as a car, but it would go faster than a red panda could run.

The wind blurred her vision, and the whining of the electric motor filled her ears. The panda dashed forward on the sidewalk. Was it moving faster? How fast did red pandas run?

Every time she'd seen them at the zoo, they were sleeping.

How can it run this fast? Is it part cheetah?

They'd barely passed Fourth Street when another dog in a yard came charging out at the panda. It spooked and scrambled and dashed down an unnamed side street toward Hillside.

"No, no, no!" Reena leaned into the sharp turn and barely missed the curb.

But the detour slowed it down. Reena pushed the battery on her little engine as the panda stumbled and tried to regain its stride.

Closer.

Closer!

She almost had it!

The panda darted in front of her with impossible agility, avoiding her front tire and vaulting onto the bumper of a parked car in the street.

"Wait!" Reena shouted after it.

The panda wasn't listening.

A school-bus-yellow Camaro with black racing stripes zoomed past them on the street, and the panda didn't even hesitate. It leaped off a parked car and landed on the roof.

The Camaro veered onto Hillside and gunned the engine in a plume of exhaust.

"Bad, very bad!" Reena added speed to her already-straining engine and checked for cross traffic before she shot across the intersection.

Ahead of her, the Camaro with the panda on its roof swung westward on to Central.

That was even worse. How was she going to catch up to them? Her engine would burn up.

Back streets.

The only option.

She skirted the Starbucks, the Spangles, and the strip mall on the other side of Wesley Hospital. Her little engine whirred and whined, but it wasn't squealing yet. Squealing was bad.

She increased the output again.

"God, don't let anybody jump out in front of me!"

She raced down the back street and glanced to the north where the Camaro was still visible bolting down Central.

She'd crossed Erie Street when the sound of shrieking brakes and droning horns filled the air. Through the parking lots she could see traffic piling up on Central as the Camaro slammed on its brakes and sent the red panda sailing into the air.

The panda smacked into the window of a passing Q-Line trolley and hung there like the ridiculous suction-cup stuffed animal Mica had on her bedroom window.

"Oh, no."

Reena gunned her scooter to follow the trolley as it swerved to avoid the pile-up on Central and made its way downtown.

"No, no, no."

Downtown was bad. One-way streets and busy intersections and blind corners and janky sidewalks. She'd never catch up to them downtown.

Ahead of her, the panda slid down the window and

disappeared inside the trolley itself. How long until someone noticed it?

Her mind ticked away on the Q-Line stops. She'd been looking it up the other day for a party she'd been planning. Where did it go after it left East Central? Did it go back downtown?

Reena winced as a truck passed her too fast. She held her ground and stayed on the wood-paneled trolley's tail.

She could see the map in her mind. It left East Central and went—back to Douglas, right? But did it take Washington?

"Oh, please let it take Washington!"

Reena steadied her scooter and reached for the visor she kept on top of her helmet. She lowered it over her eyes and tapped the boot-up button on the arm.

A HUD screen filled with data over her left eye.

She and Jim had designed it a few months back as part of a research project, trying to translate the functionality of the Peregrine wrist watches into a visor. It hadn't turned out nearly as practical as they'd hoped, but she'd kept the prototype.

"ROM, I need a hand."

The screen flashed a smiley face emoji at her.

Strictly speaking, ROM was the artificial intelligence interface Peregrine Agents used on their cases. It wasn't for personal use. But Jim had loaded some of ROM's programming into the visor as a test, and Reena simply hadn't removed it yet.

"Give me the readout of the Wichita Q-Line trolley route. I need where it is and where it's going." She peered through the visor text to the trolley's service number. "Trolley number seven."

ROM flashed a thumbs up emoji at her and in moments listed out a detailed route, including stops.

Trolley 7 was an express route, which made a run between Central and Volutsia and didn't stop until it hit Douglas and Washington.

"Aha!"

It was the best possible option in the worst-case scenario.

"ROM, I need you to send a text." Reena corrected her angle to get around a pothole. "Mica Sherman."

ROM flashed a question mark.

"Skipping lunch. Need help now," Reena dictated with a smirk. "Hope you brought your helmet to work."

As her scooter whirred along the road, keeping the trolley in sight, Reena grinned when the visor screen flashed again with a line of text from her best friend.

"Don't I always?"

3

s the red brick buildings of Old Town came into view, Reena shifted forward on her scooter, making as much room at the back of the running board as possible.

The last time Mica tried to jump aboard as Reena passed, it hadn't exactly worked.

But no bones were broken. No stitches needed. So it wasn't a complete, failure, right?

It had to work this time. Reena didn't have time to stop fully and build up momentum again, and she needed Mica's help.

Up ahead a few more blocks, a stoplight hovered threateningly above the intersection of Central and Washington. They'd have to hit it just right.

Her visor flashed, and the screen displayed a photograph of an older blond teenager with blue eyes making a terrible face at the camera.

Reena caught her breath.

Because of course Jim would call her right now.

I need to talk to him, but why couldn't he wait for me to call him?

The stupid picture of his face mocked her.

If she didn't pick up, he'd know something was wrong.

Fine.

She gave one quick nod to accept the call, and Jim's voice greeted her faintly in the Bluetooth earpiece she'd soldered into her helmet. "Hey, Reena!"

"Hi, Jim!" Reena forced herself to sound cheerful and calm. "How are you doing?"

"What's wrong?" Jim went deadpan immediately.

"Nothing!" She squeaked and stifled a groan as she hit a pothole that nearly threw her. "I'm cheerful and calm."

"Reena."

And now he was pulling the big brother voice. Jim didn't really know how to be a big brother, since he'd only ever been a little brother, but at least he was trying.

"Everything's fine, Jim. You just caught me in the middle of something."

"Are you—driving?" His voice took on the same tone her mother's voice did when she found her husband in the kitchen making dinner.

Knowing Jim, he was already running a satellite scan of her location.

"Reena, your scooter isn't rated for city driving!"

Wow, that didn't take him long at all.

"I'm fine."

"You're really not. You need to get off the street right now."

"I will, I will." She dodged another pothole. "I just really need to pick up something, and I'll go right home. I promise."

He sighed heavily.

He must have been practicing his authentic-sounding big brother sighs, because that one was pretty convincing.

"Can I call you back later so we can talk when I'm not distracted?" She forced the cheerful and calm tone again. "You always tell me not to get distracted when I'm driving.

"You're going to make me old, Reena."

"You're already old."

The trolley was turning. She adjusted her stance on the scooter and followed it around the corner as the light turned yellow behind her.

"Okay," Jim started, "well, I was going to call about the exam. But you're right. We should talk about that when you aren't distracted. But there was something else too."

"Mm-hmm."

"So, remember a couple weeks ago when we kind of opened a door into an alternate dimension?"

Reena rolled her eyes. "No, Jim, I completely forgot about that."

"You did?"

"Jim, how is it you speak twenty languages, and you don't understand sarcasm?"

"So, you do remember?"

"Yes, I remember falling into an alternate dimension, Jim,"

Reena huffed as she scooted roughly over a patched crack in the road. "I remember the talking fox people and the centaurs and the random alien people who eat Indian food."

"Oh, good, you do remember."

They were really going to have to work on that. He understood his sister, and Barb had a doctorate in sarcasm. This shouldn't be difficult for him and his very literal brain.

"I had you running a keyword search in the Peregrine archives for any reference to the Mitchell case back in the late 90s, or the 2000s," Jim said. "Did you get that started?"

"Yeah, right away." Reena guided her scooter up on the sidewalk as the road turned to bricks. No way was she driving her scooter over bricks. She'd break her teeth.

"Okay, I need you to put a halt on that," Jim said, his voice turning just a bit sharp. "Kind of fast."

"Why? Did something happen to Meg or her family?"

Jim cleared his throat. "Oh, just found some new information." His voice sounded a bit higher than normal. "Not a big deal. We don't need the Peregrine archives anymore."

Even as she shot down Washington street in pursuit of the Q-Line trolley with the wind blasting her face and the whir of her engine ringing in her ears, she could hear the lie in his voice.

Jim was lying to her.

And now she was really curious.

She dodged a person who was standing on the sidewalk talking into a cell phone.

Jim never lied to her. Ever.

Something big must have happened. I hope Jenny is okay.

But as much as she cared about the new friends she'd made in the Andarian Dimension, she didn't have time to think about them right then. She'd think about it later. After the marauding pink-red panda was no longer in danger of terrorizing the city.

"You got it, Jim," she said.

"And you can do it today?"

"Sure can."

"Great." He sounded relieved. "And you're going to get off the street, right?"

"Already am!"

She neglected to mention that she'd be back on the street again in a few moments, but what Jim didn't need to know wouldn't hurt him.

"Okay." He paused. "And you know I'm really proud of you, right? That you don't have to pass an exam for me to think you're the greatest?"

Tears burned in her eyes and blinked them away fiercely. "Yeah, I know, Jim."

He cleared his throat. "Good. I just—wanted you to know. Being the smartest or the strongest isn't all it's cracked up to be. Just be good at what you're good at. Okay?"

"Okay. Thanks, Jim." She sniffled gratefully.

"Be careful out there, you little punk."

Reena smirked. "I will if you will, you big nerd."

Jim laughed. "Later." And he hung up.

Reena blew out an exhausted breath and gunned the engine. She'd figure out what Jim was talking about later and made a mental note to discontinue the keyword search as soon as she survived this current crisis.

Second Street was approaching. Things were going to get real hairy real fast because the trolley wasn't going to stop, and Reena had to divert to pick up Mica.

She could cut across the intersection and zoom into the parking lot where Mica would be waiting, and then they could follow the trolley as it continued down Washington toward Douglas.

Except—

The trolley suddenly veered sharply across traffic and then back again, wobbling and wiggling as it came up to the intersection. Reena could hear screaming inside.

"Oh no."

Sure enough, the red panda clambered out of the back window, wide-eyed and frantic to escape the inside of the trolley.

"No, no, come on!"

The panda leaped off the trolley and landed in the bed of a passing pickup truck. The truck turned on Second Street and zoomed west toward the river.

"Okay, doesn't change the plan." Reena sped up and gauged the oncoming traffic. It wasn't going to be a problem.

She sailed across the intersection diagonally and aimed for the parking lot of Senjumin sushi restaurant.

Out front of the restaurant, Mica bounced up and down in the parking lot, waving her hands over her head like a maniac. Her golden yellow leggings blurred vibrantly in the shade of the brick restaurant, topped off with denim shorts and a slouchy forest-green Henley that was probably two sizes too big.

Since it was Mica, she probably had a paisley print duster somewhere too, but fortunately she'd left it behind. And, as promised, she was already wearing her helmet—a lime green job plastered with vinyl bumblebee stickers.

Reena glided past her and Mica broke into a run, picking up speed until she was able to leap off the sidewalk and land on the back of the scooter board, holding on to Reena for support.

"Hey, that worked!" Mica laughed.

"Yeah, for once." Reena gunned it and chased after the truck.

"Did you see that?" Mica took hold of the steering bar under Reena's arms and held on. "That little critter? It jumped right off the trolley."

"I saw it."

"That's what we're after, right?"

"It's in the blue truck up ahead."

"Awwww." Mica cooed. "What's her name? She's so fluffy and pink."

"She's a menace."

"You're just grumpy 'cause you've been chasing her all this time. I bet she's scared of you. I bet she'll like me just fine."

Reena checked the traffic before scooting across the next

intersection. The speed limit on Second Street was slower than Washington, and the old blue truck ahead of them kept belching out smoke. Maybe they would actually be able to catch it.

"You found it in your dad's office?"

"It hatched out of that old geode on Dad's shelf."

"Whoa. Where did he get it? And where can I get one just like it?"

Reena rolled her eyes and got them across another intersection.

"Thanks for helping," Reena shouted back at her.

"Are you kidding? What are besties for?"

Reena smirked and poured on the speed while Mica clung to her waist, grinning like they were off on a grand adventure.

Mica was the variety of maniac everyone needed to protect their lives from boredom.

Reena had every possible strike against her on the Friend Scale. Her dad worked for the FBI, and for some reason that intimidated everybody. Reena was smart enough to have been hired by the Peregrine Agency, which meant to everybody else that she was too smart to be normal. And Reena herself just wasn't cool. Cecelia got all the looks. Her older brother Tayvian got all the athleticism. Sure, she got all the smarts, but that was the least useful skill in having friends when you were fourteen.

But that's not how Mica made friends.

Mica just looked for whoever seemed lonely and attached herself until you pried her off with a crowbar.

"Hey, Reena?"

"What?"

"We're going to go past Epic Center."

Reena blinked at her and then at the tall building up ahead of them.

"Oh boy."

Of all the buildings they were going to pass, why did they have to go past Epic Center? Her dad's FBI field office was on the fourth floor of the Epic Center, and if one of his coworkers happened to notice the ridiculous pink red panda causing chaos outside, it would absolutely get back to him.

Ahead of them, the blue truck stuttered and coughed, and the little creature in the bed poked its furry head up over the tailgate.

"What's she doing?" Mica gasped.

Reena increased the speed. "I think she's jumping out."

The little pink red panda gathered itself and leaped out of the truck bed. She sailed through the air and hit the sidewalk at the intersection of Second and Main in a rolled-up ball of striped fur. She crashed into one of the bushes and scrambled out the other side.

"Reena." Mica caught her breath.

"I see it. I see it."

Reena increased the speed.

If even one of the other FBI agents saw the panda and Reena chasing it, they'd have so much explaining to do. Like why they didn't just call for help instead of chasing the panda themselves?

That's actually a really good question. Reena sighed to

herself. *I'll have to come up with a really good reason for why this seemed like a good idea at the time.*

Reena popped the scooter up on the curb just as the red panda darted through the revolving doors into the atrium of the tallest building in Kansas.

Mica jumped off the back of the scooter as Reena parked it and turned the engine to idle. They ran after the panda. The cafe inside the atrium wasn't open, so no one was visible at the tables or waiting for the elevators, fortunately.

But one of the stairwell doors was propped open, and that's where the red panda went.

"Are we taking the stairs?" Mica groaned.

"We have to!" Reena raced after the red panda.

"There are a million stories, Reena!" Mica followed her as they hit the cement steps and began the trek upward toward the twenty-second floor.

Their hurried footfalls echoed in the cement stairwell, and the cold cast iron banister railing felt icy under Reena's hand.

Just get past the fourth floor. Just get past the fourth floor.

She and Mica dashed up the stairs on floor four and kept going, and Reena breathed a little easier. If any of her father's FBI coworkers had come out into the stairwell, there would have been trouble.

Well, more trouble.

They circled and circled and circled. Ahead of them the panda did the same until they all began to falter.

Halfway up, the jumping red panda ahead of them wasn't jumping anymore. Even from a floor and a half behind it, Reena could hear the little creature grunting and gasping.

"Maybe--we'll get lucky and--it'll run--out of steam." Mica gasped.

"We're not that lucky," Reena panted.

They climbed.

And climbed.

And climbed.

Reena stumbled up the stairs, refusing to quit. Mica dragged herself behind her.

Floor twenty.

Floor twenty-one.

Floor twenty-two! Finally!

"Won't the door be locked?" Mica struggled for air on the half stair leading up to the top landing.

Reena pointed to the propped open door that led to the roof. "I told you. No luck. At all."

Mica groaned and followed Reena onto the roof.

Epic Center's roof had a narrow ledge that ran the perimeter of the building, and the triangular-shaped rooftop had been formed from copper. It practically glowed in the bright sunshine.

Reena shaded her eyes.

It was possible to get to the peak of the roof, but it wasn't easy. And hopefully the panda hadn't figured it out because Reena wasn't sure how to get up there.

"Reena." Mica grabbed her arm and pointed.

In the corner of the roof, the little red panda curled into a ball, gasping and shivering against the ledge. Reena lifted her visor and approached the animal softly, with her hands spread.

"Hey, little one." Reena crept toward it. "I know you're scared. Come on. With me. I'll take you home, okay?"

The animal went wide-eyed again, bristling and posturing.

Mica stopped Reena with a hand on her shoulder. "Maybe we need to prove that we're friends."

Reena sighed. "How are we supposed to do that? I'm talking to it, aren't I?"

"You can't always convince someone you're friendly by talking." Mica beamed. "Sometimes you have to bribe them." She shoved her hand into her jeans pocket and pulled out a plastic sack of pickled ginger. "See?"

Reena wrinkled her nose. "What are you going to do with that nasty stuff?"

"It's delicious."

"That's a matter of opinion."

Mica harrumphed. "You don't know what's good, you heathen." She stepped around Reena and inched toward the panda.

"Hi." She knelt. "I'm Mica. You don't know me, but I think we're going to be friends. Even if you're pink. Pink is an okay color, but I like yellow better."

The red panda tilted her head at Mica's voice, pink irises showing a bit more color than before as its pupils began to retract.

Reena held her breath.

Did red pandas like pickled ginger? What was this madness?

Well, if that was the case, maybe they could lure it close enough for her to touch it. If she could grab it and get it in her backpack, they could get it home in one piece before her dad knew any of this had happened.

Mica opened the plastic bag of ginger and smelled it. She pulled out a tiny sliver of the obnoxiously scented, pinkish-colored root and waved it at the red panda.

"See?" She ate the piece of pickled ginger and grinned. "It's yummy. And so good for your digestion too."

"Yes, we want to make sure the marauding red panda is getting all her probiotic fiber." Reena rolled her eyes.

The red panda began to sniff the air, bristled tail bushing out behind her.

Incredible.

This might actually work.

But how to catch the creature?

Reena peeled her backpack off. "You keep doing whatever you're doing." She backed away. "I'll go around and come up behind her."

Mica gave her a thumbs up.

Reena turned on her heel and started jogging around the roof's ledge. It was a large building, but it wouldn't take her too long to make the whole circuit and come up the other side behind the red panda.

They could do this.

She could still catch it and get it home before her dad found out. This was going to work. It had to work.

The gravel on top of the Epic Center roof crunched under Reena's tennis shoes as she crouched below the line of the concrete ledge that lined the perimeter. It blocked some of the wind too.

Before her, the bristled red panda had taken two steps toward Mica and her proffered pickled ginger. So, red pandas *did* eat pickled ginger. Who knew?

Mental note. More research.

How was she going to do this? She was hidden now, but the instant she rushed the little creature, it would run. It would jump on the ledge and prance away, and Mica? Well, Mica wasn't exactly the most coordinated person in the world. Actually, other than Jim, Mica was the clumsiest person Reena had ever met.

The instant Mica pursued the red panda, she'd trip and fall off the building.

So, startling it was a no go.

Reena paused, watching in silence as the little red panda eagerly ate the strip of pickled ginger Mica offered. The bristling of its fur calmed, and Mica cooed and clapped her hands joyfully.

"Isn't that tasty?" Mica laughed. "I knew you'd like it."

The red panda ate some more, happily munching away. It stood on its back paws and used both front paws to shove more ginger in its mouth.

So much for what I know. Reena smirked to herself.

The little panda was so focused on Mica and its pickled ginger treat, maybe it wouldn't notice Reena sneaking up behind it now.

Reena crept around the corner and slid toward the happily snacking red panda, its pink fur no longer bristled.

"You are so cute," Mica was saying, her voice muffled by the wind. "I don't know where you came from, but I hope you stick around. If you stick around, I'll smuggle you as much pickled ginger as I can sneak out under Uncle Fox's nose."

Mica kept babbling.

She did that with animals. But then she did that with people too. If the average female woman had 50,000 words to speak in a day as the old research study declared, Mica had twice that.

The gravel crunched and rustled, but the red panda didn't notice. It was too focused on Mica and her constant chatter.

A perfect distraction.

This is going to work! It's really going to work!

Reena crept closer. She brought her backpack around and unzipped it quietly. All she'd have to do is grab the little red panda by the back of its neck and shove it in her bag. Mica would help her get it closed, and then they could go home.

Easy peasy, lemon squeezy.

She was three feet away. The red panda hadn't taken its eyes off Mica yet, and Mica gave it the last of the pickled ginger.

It's now or never.

Reena closed her eyes and calmed her nerves. Months and months earlier, Barb had coached her through an obstacle course at Peregrine HQ. Precise motion was directly proportional to sufficient oxygen. Most people didn't breathe deeply enough, and that couldn't be the case with a Peregrine agent in the field.

Peregrine agents couldn't make mistakes.

She inhaled. Deeply.

She exhaled, long and slow.

And she opened her eyes to focus on her target, the cheerful little red panda with its twitching pink-and-maroon striped tail.

Reena lunged.

She seized the scruff at the back of the red panda's neck— and time stopped. As though the world had frozen mid-spin. The wind disappeared. Mica disappeared, and so did the Epic Center.

Reena's vision blurred and jolted violently, and she was kneeling in a darkened throne room. Elegant marble floor tiles cracked and shattered, stained with dark blood and strewn with glass that reflected the light like shards of broken mirrors.

The air froze her lungs. It smelled of copper and burning wires and death. Her toes and fingers felt numb, stiff, the throb of a deep wound somewhere in her chest aching.

What is this? What's happening?

Before her, in the dark, an ornate throne stood on a raised platform. It sparkled in spite of the shadows, studded with diamonds, but no one sat on it.

A hand on her shoulder.

Reena turned her gaze and looked up into the terrified features of a face she knew well. The face had watched over their dining room table at home as long as Reena had been alive.

Eedo Hani? Reena whispered, her voice echoing in the dark.

What was her father's sister doing here? The woman's mouth moved, but no sound came out. Blood dribbled down the side of her face, trickling between the short twists of her dark hair.

Light, blinding light, seared Reena's eyes, and the whole room shook with a distant explosion. Jagged sections of the ceiling tumbled through the air and erupted against the broken tile floor in showers of shrapnel.

Her father's sister scooped her up and carried her close to her chest.

But how is that possible? She can't carry me. Reena swallowed the panic rising in her throat as the whole world shook and fell apart around them. *And she's dead. She died years ago.*

Reena glanced down at her chest where the low ache of hemorrhaging had begun to grow cold. Her chest felt hard, like stone. The wound over her heart had begun to solidify, turning from flesh into rock.

What kind of nightmare is this?

A powerful thrust launched her backward so hard that she

crashed against the copper-plated roof of the Epic Center pyramid. She gasped for breath like she hadn't tasted oxygen in years.

She was back in Wichita. Back on top of Epic Center with the dry wind tossing her braids and the sharp gravel poking the back of her legs.

But the little red panda was gone.

Before her, on the roof of Epic Center towered a sparkling, pink dragon. Thirty feet long from the tip of its snout to the end of its spike-covered tail. Its tail thrashed against the blue sky, and it opened its crocodile mouth to roar over the deafening wind.

Reena gawked until her mouth felt dry.

What was this?

What had happened?

Where had the red panda gone?

What was that vision?

The dragon arched its neck and shrieked, a sound somewhere between the distant rumble of thunder and the high-pitched dissonance of the wind chimes on their porch.

It shook its rhinoceros-like body, scattered iridescent scales along its spine and sides and flanks sparkling like pink prisms in the sunlight.

Wings. It has wings.

Of course it had wings. It was a dragon. How was it a dragon?

The beast braced to unfurl its massive wings, and Reena screamed, reaching out for Mica who stood to the side of the dragon.

Right next to the ledge of the roof.

"Mica!" Reena grabbed for her.

"Reena!"

The dragon snapped open leathery pink wings that stretched sixty feet wide, beating the sky. The monstrous power of its wings flung Mica over the ledge and into the air.

Reena dashed to the ledge. "Mica!"

Her red-headed friend screeched in utter panic, tumbling end-over-end through the fierce winds toward the unyielding asphalt of Third and Main.

No, no, no, no—

The building shifted. Not with the wind. With the weight of the giant pink dragon.

Reena choked on her breath as a massive talon seized her off the roof. The dragon snatched her off her feet, pulling her close to its chest, and dove into the wind.

They fell so fast, Reena's eyes watered. Or maybe she was crying. She couldn't tell.

She reached out her hands toward Mica's tumbling body. Mica's carrot-colored hair frizzed out around her terrified face, so pale her freckles looked like ants.

The whistling wind carried Mica's screams away.

We won't make it! We won't catch her in time!

Gravity dragged them downward relentlessly, but Mica had fallen first. And Epic Center wasn't that tall.

The giant pink dragon flapped its wings and thrust them forward.

Somehow the air smelled of cut grass and fresh pastries from the vegan restaurant across the street. The sunlight flashed on the car windshields in the Epic Center parking lot.

Had panic turned everything to slow motion?

The dragon turned in the air, catching a wild breeze from above them, funneled between the tall downtown buildings, and tucked its wings tight against its body.

The dragon snatched Mica out of the air and unfurled its massive wings.

The whiplash drove the air out of Reena's lungs with a violent jarring sensation. The dragon sailed upward toward the sky, banking and twisting to avoid the downtown buildings.

Mica's screaming choked off with the force of the dragon's motion.

The dragon's mighty wings pulled them higher and higher and higher, above the top of Epic Center before it spread them to their full width and soared away from the city.

The air was frigid, but the dragon's skin burned under Reena's hands.

"Mica!" Reena shouted.

Mica clung to the dragon's talons, gazing up at her with a wide-eyed expression like a suffocating catfish.

Reena clung to the dragon's talon and tried to change position, but the dragon tightened its grip. She started to shout, but a powerful pulse of energy jolted down her spine. Her vision blurred again.

Fire surrounded them, burning fierce and bright and glorious. The Darksiders didn't stand a chance against the furious inferno Bast had laid down between them and the royal family.

Bast? Reena tried to breathe through the heat. *Who is Bast?*

The world looked different again. Still dark, but the shadows glittered with refracted light. And everything seemed so much smaller than before.

She looked down.

Eedo Hani! Again, her father's sister stood at her side, but she was tiny. How had she gotten so small? Had she shrunk?

Her aunt grinned up at her, the same expression on the painted portrait that hung over their dinner table at home. Confident and jovial, a sparkle in her dark eyes.

And she wore—armor?

Shining plated armor hung from her shoulders, her hips, and protected her back and chest. It gleamed in pink and rose hues, intertwined with bronze and silver.

"That should hold them, Bast." Eedo Hani nodded at her. "Let's find the princess." She pulled a helmet shaped like the dragon's face out from under her arm and settled it over the spiky twists on her head.

The world spun around them.

Reena's heart lodged in her throat. *Why is this happening? Is it the dragon?* But how could it be the dragon? What happened to the fluffy red panda?

Mumbling voices echoed in her ears, exclamations of delight and the warbling of praise songs far in the background.

She opened her eyes to gaze into Eedo Hani's face.

Young.

She was so young.

Eedo Hani whispered something in Somalian, cradling Reena close to her, holding her tightly. Gentle hands fell on both of them, voices raised in excitement and joy.

Eedo Hani beamed down at her.

The air felt colder than it had before. So cold that even the warmth of the dragon's skin couldn't reach her. Had the wind gotten louder?

"Reena!" Mica had begun to shout.

She sounded so far away.

The dragon's grip on her tightened further, and a low rumbling began deep in its throat. The cold world around them jolted and shifted again, going dark.

So dark.

So dark inside the prison. No escape. No way out.

And then, the walls began to crack. The prison walls sheered apart and began to drop away. Light speared across the darkness. The air smelled of dust. So different from the world as it had been.

And there was a girl.

A scrawny little thing in vibrant pink and purple clothes, long braids draping down her back and shoulders. Big dark eyes blinked in surprise.

"A red panda?" the girl stared rudely. "Or a pink panda? A pink red panda?"

That's me. Reena realized numbly. *I'm staring at myself. But how—is this how the red panda saw me? Am I seeing from the red panda's eyes?*

The steel-boned grip of the dragon's talon around Reena's chest tightened even further before the beast shuddered in mid-flight. Reena shook herself out of the vision.

Wichita was gone.

"Reena!" Mica screamed. "Are you awake?"

Reena looked over at her friend, dizziness washing over her in a wave of exhaustion.

Mica waved her arms with short, shaky motions. "Wake up! We're gonna crash!"

I just need to sleep. Reena's eyes tried to close. *Why am I so tired? It's like all my energy is gone.*

She tried to hold to the dragon's talon, but her fingers stopped working. Her head throbbed with the effort of staying up.

We're falling.

She tried to breathe, but her lungs wouldn't inflate.

Why are we falling?

"Reena!" Mica screamed again.

Reena wrapped her arms around the dragon's talon and clung to it, laying her head along the nearest claw.

I don't know who you are. I don't know what you want.

Reena closed her eyes. *You're a dragon. A real-life dragon. So, fly. Fly a little further.*

She was so tired.

How had she gotten so tired so fast?

A warm pulse threaded through her mind, as comforting as her mother's arms around her shoulders.

Forgive me, little one. A deep voice resonated in her mind. *But I need your strength a moment longer.*

Who had spoken?

Who'd said that?

Reena lifted her eyes to the dragon's face, expression set on the clear horizon ahead as it dropped them ever closer to the ground.

Was that you? Did you—speak?

Reena's ears popped as the air pressure shifted. The wind howled and wailed in her ears so loudly she couldn't hear anything but the throbbing of the dragon's heart. Calm and consistent.

She focused on it, the only sound in her ears.

If the dragon were scared, wouldn't its heart have been beating faster? Maybe that was a good sign. Maybe the dragon was still in control after all.

So tired.

She yawned.

She should be panicking. Her mom would have been panicking. Cecelia certainly would have been.

But panic wasn't her style. And what good would panicking do anyway? It might scare the dragon, and right now, only the dragon could save them.

Reena grunted as the world shifted again. Something shook her, a powerful jolt. Whatever energy she'd had drained out of her like melted candle wax.

A nap wouldn't hurt, would it?

Maybe when she woke up, she could learn the dragon's name and how the dragon knew her father's sister. Even she didn't know Eedo Hani, except from photos.

The dragon's talon tightened a little bit more, and the rush of wind changed to the scrape of leaves and branches against leathery scales.

Rest, amiirad. The voice rumbled in her mind. *And forgive me.*

6

Reena."

Cold fingers clutched at her wrist.

"Reena? Reena, please wake up. Please be okay."

The air smelled like grass. Grass and muddy water.

Warm winds stirred the stray hairs of her braids across her forehead.

Her eyelids felt like they weighed as much as the bags of dog food Hermes consumed every month.

"Mica?" she whispered.

Mica exhaled heavily and clung tighter to her wrist. "You're awake. Are you okay? Oh, Reena, that was insane."

"What happened?"

"Don't move!" Mica pressed her hands against her shoulders. "I mean, I don't think you should move. I don't know. I don't know anything anymore."

"I need to sit up."

"You passed out, Reena." Mica sighed. "You went all rigid and stuff. And you're still all pale and clammy."

Reena arched an eyebrow at her. "Am I as pale as you?"

Mica scowled at her. "If you ever go as pale as me, I'll just assume you died."

"If I'm ever as pale as you, that's a valid assumption." Reena held out her hand. "Help me up."

Mica pulled her to a seated position, and Reena waited until her eyes stopped spinning in their sockets to look around.

They sat in the freshly mowed grass of a hill in Riverside Park. It was a place Reena often visited when she went for lunch with her father downtown.

"How did we get here?"

Mica raised her red eyebrows. "You don't remember?"

Reena blinked at her and glanced just over her shoulder to where the fluffy red panda from her father's office stared at them with white eyebrows drawn together over its snout.

"Oh." Reena sagged her face into her hands. "Well, I remember something, but I thought I was tripping."

"You're telling me." Mica sat next to her.

"I remember—" Reena stopped.

"A dragon." Mica nodded. "It was a big, pink, sparkling dragon. And it knocked me off the roof and then it caught us both and we crashed here."

Reena looked around. "Where did the dragon go?"

Mica huffed and pointed at the red panda. "There's the culprit."

"Seriously?"

"Seriously. It turned into the dragon, Reena."

"How?"

"Hey, you're the genius, interdimensional-hopping, alien-friend person." Mica snorted. "You tell me."

Reena gazed at the red panda, who sat calmly before them, twitching its tail.

"When I touched it, on the Epic Center roof, I saw something," she said.

"What?" Mica scooted closer.

"I don't really know," Reena said. "I was in a different place. A dark place. And I was with Eedo Hani."

"Your dad's sister?"

Reena nodded. "She was alive and young and strong." She shook her head. "Not like I ever saw her. Like she was in the photos from when she came to America from Somalia."

The red panda tilted its furry face and spoke. "Your father's sister did not come from any place called Somalia."

Reena scowled.

Mica cocked her head to the side and wrinkled her nose. "Huh?"

They both stared at the pink-and-maroon striped red panda, which had so obviously opened its snout full of needle-sharp teeth and spoke with a deep male voice.

"Reena?" Mica gawked. "Did it just—?"

"Talk?" Reena's mouth hung open.

The red panda looked at Mica and then at Reena and spoke again. "Your father's sister did not come from Somalia or any nation on this world."

Reena fixed her eyes on the talking red panda and scrambled to reach her backpack, digging for the can of mace inside.

Mica leaned forward, gaping at the creature. "You talk?"

The red panda settled back on its haunches and folded its arms, striped tail twitching more violently. "Yes, I talk."

Mica gripped her head. "This is crazy. We're talking to a red panda."

"No, you're talking to a red panda." Reena pulled out her can of mace. "Either we're crazy, or it's possessed." She aimed at the creature.

The red panda rolled its round eyes and sighed hugely. "Ugh, this is going to take a lot of work."

"You stay over there, or I'll blast you!" Reena brandished the mace threateningly.

"Reena, he hasn't hurt anybody." Mica settled next to her again.

"He knocked you off the Epic Center!"

"That was an accident." Mica shrugged.

"If it could talk, it should have talked sooner!"

"Maybe he forgot how." Mica patted Reena's knee. "Let's give him a chance to explain, since he can. Can't say that about every red panda I've ever met."

"You've never met a red panda."

Mica grinned. "Exactly."

"Did you hit your head on the way down?"

Mica felt her scalp. "I don't think so."

Reena huffed and lowered the mace. "Fine." She gestured broadly to the red panda that was staring at them skeptically. "Talk. But if I don't like what I hear, I'm blasting you."

The red panda glanced between them again. "Your strange little pale friend is right, *amiirad*. I did not remember who I was, and I did not know who you were until we touched."

The red panda pitched forward and approached on four legs. Once he sat in front of Reena, he curled into a ball, muttering something under his breath. When he unfolded, he held a shimmering pink jewel in his paws.

"The Heart of Arawelo." He held it out to her. "It rightfully belongs to you."

"Whoa," Mica whispered.

Reena reached out her hand to take the glowing pink jewel. It was the size of a quarter, and the instant her fingertips brushed it, the jewel ignited with brilliant rose-colored light. It glittered and sparkled in her palm, sending warmth radiating up her arm and all through her body.

"Wow," she breathed. "What—what is this?"

"The Heart of Arawelo. Aren't you listening?" The red panda curled its lip at her.

"That means nothing to me." Reena raised her eyebrows at it. "And you still haven't told me why I shouldn't mace you. I don't even know your name."

The red panda smirked.

Could red pandas smirk? Apparently they could, because the little creature's expression mimicked a human's so closely it could have been human itself.

"I am Bast. And you will soon understand."

The pink jewel in Reena's hand sparkled more brightly, as though fireworks were erupting beneath its facets. Shivering electricity jolted up Reena's arm, arcing through her shoulders, her breath caught in her throat.

"Reena!" Mica shrieked.

Reena grunted as Mica flung her arms around her, and a blast of blinding light surrounded them. Reena squeezed her eyes shut against the brightness, but her eyelids couldn't block out the light. Her whole body tingled, like she had become the inside of the pink jewel. And somewhere in the back of her mind, she sensed the red panda's amusement.

When the light faded, it left cold air. The grass beneath her had vanished, replaced with chilly metal floors. And either the heat from the light had truly blinded her, or there was no light around them.

"Reena?" Mica whispered.

"Mica?" Reena blinked her eyes. "I can't see you."

"I can't see you either."

Okay. So, no lights here. Either that or Mica's blind too. Isn't that a cheerful thought?

Reena held on to Mica's arm as the girl unfolded herself from around her, but in the darkness, she couldn't identify any details.

"Where are we?" Mica's voice echoed in the room. "Where did the critter go?"

"Bast, right?" Reena mumbled. "Bast?"

The red panda didn't answer. The cold air around them seemed to grow colder.

"I don't like this, Mica," Reena said. "I don't like this."

"I don't like it either." Mica tightened her grip on Reena's elbow. "How did you do—whatever you did?"

"I have no idea." Reena lifted her arm and uncurled her fingers from around the shimmering jewel in her hand. Pink light washed over them both, bathing Mica's pale face in a rose-tinted glow.

"Can you do it again?" Mica grimaced.

"I don't know how I did it to begin with, Mica."

Little toenails skittered across the metal floor, and Bast scurried back up to them, his eyebrows raised and his eyes wide.

"This is wrong," his voice sounded panicked. "This is all wrong." He jumped into Reena's lap and put his nose nearly against hers. "What year is it? What year?"

"It's 2010," Reena said. "Why?"

"No, on the Inyangan calendar!" Bast said fiercely. "What year of the Inyangan calendar?"

"What's an Inyangan calendar?" Mica whispered.

"No clue."

Bast groaned dramatically and sagged as though he had sand

for filling. "How is this possible? How can we be here? This isn't the palace!"

Reena patted the top of his head. "What palace?"

He swatted her hand away grumpily. "Don't you know anything? The palace! The Kiti Almasi! The seat of authority for the entirety of Inyanga Bukhosi!"

Reena and Mica exchanged a look, and Reena shivered in the cold air. They needed to figure out where they were, and Bast wasn't helping.

Bast turned in Reena's lap and crawled back up to her face again, staring at her. "You are the daughter of the Great Lady Hanihaweeyo, the Dragon of Arawelo. How can you know nothing of Inyanga Bukhosi or the Queen Under the Moon?" His voice shook.

Reena lifted her hand. "My mom is named Ellie. FYI."

"Do you understand anything he's saying?" Mica whispered.

"I have no idea what he's talking about," Reena said.

"I'm sitting right here." Bast folded his little arms again. "I can hear you."

"Yeah, and I still have my mace." Reena waggled the aerosol can again.

The red panda sighed. "Your ancestors will change the wind for this. What has your mother taught you?" The animal crawled onto Reena's leg and into her lap. "Take me to her."

Reena, frozen with surprise at the furry red panda in her lap, stuttered. "My mom? My what? Why?"

"The Great Lady Hanihaweeyo has failed in her duty somehow." The red panda nodded. "She has not prepared you. I will speak with her and rectify this unfortunate situation."

Mica giggled. "He's so cute."

"That's not helping, Mica." Reena rolled her eyes.

"But he is."

Reena looked down at the creature in her lap. "Look, can we talk about my mom later? It's freezing in here, and I don't know where we are."

The fur along Bast's spine stood up as he reared back on his hind legs and lifted his little snout. "This is the *Ikroza*, where the wandering stars gather. You should know it." He snorted. "But it is wrong. It is dark and cold, and it should be alive."

He climbed off Reena's lap and stood in the pink-hued light from the jewel. His bushy tail twitched.

"I fear something is terribly wrong," he murmured. "Something horrible has happened."

Furious red light flared to life all around them, and a deafening alarm warbled loud enough to vibrate the floors. Reena cried out and covered her ears as the noise rattled her eardrums.

"What is it?" Mica screamed.

Bast spun in a circle, furry face horrified. "Lock down. Why is it locking down?"

In the flashing red lights, Reena could finally make out the details of the room. She and Mica sat on the floor at the center of a giant metal chamber. Every burst of red light revealed a huge computer system built into the far wall, a massive viewing screen with multiple panels and keyboards attached to it.

"A computer." Reena pitched forward and ran toward it. "Finally, something that makes sense."

"What are you doing?" Mica followed her, shouting over the alarm.

"We can keep sitting there asking questions that Bast isn't answering, or we can figure it out for ourselves." Reena started tapping buttons on the computer panels.

Bast scurried across the floor and climbed onto the main panel. "My lady, you don't understand." He grabbed her wrist. "The *Ikroza* will eject us. The security systems are following their protocols. If we do not stop the countdown, all atmosphere in the station will be emptied. We will suffocate."

Reena stared at the red panda.

"Well, let's not do that," Mica said.

"Right," Reena nodded. "Let's not do that. How do we shut it off?"

Bast's grim expression didn't change, and Reena's stomach fell.

He didn't know. Bast didn't know how to stop it. They would suffocate, and she didn't know how to stop it.

Reena squared her jaw. "Everybody, start pushing buttons. We have to wake this computer up. Bast, find me a panel I can get into." She fished the utility tool out of her shorts pocket. "If we can't wake it up, I can hotwire it."

Bast flared his nostrils. "This is the most advanced computer system in the galaxy. You think you can do to infiltrate it with a tiny little knife?"

Reena smirked. "Watch me."

The giant screen flared to life with a burst of white light.

"Aha!" Mica flung her arms over her head. "It's alive! It's alive!"

"Still not helping." Reena scrambled to the keyboard where Mica was standing. "Help Bast find a back door."

Mica saluted awkwardly and dropped to the floor, crawling under the computer system to search in the darkness for an access panel. With every burst of red light, more of the computer terminal grew in Reena's vision. Keyboards and switchers and sliders and dials and gauges—it was too much to take in at one time.

The main viewing screen shone pure white light into the chamber, and it displayed a single prompt in a language that didn't look familiar.

"Bast!" Reena called.

The little red panda crawled onto the panel and blinked at the screen.

"What language is that?" Reena asked.

"Inyangan," he said sourly. "Not that it helps you any if you know nothing about it."

Reena set the glowing pink jewel on the control panel dash and started typing on the main keyboard. Characters filled the screen, but the prompt didn't accept them. It would allow the characters, but the screen would flash and delete them all.

"This is impossible." Reena pulled on her braids. "I don't even know the language."

The jewel on the dash winked at her.

"It needs a passcode." Bast folded his furry arms.

The blinking red lights illuminated the dashboard where a u-shaped wire sparked with electricity between its two contact points. Reena glanced between it and the glowing pink jewel.

"A passcode? Or a fingerprint?" She snatched the jewel and set it in between the contact points of the fork.

Instantly, the entire computer terminal came to life. Lights hiccupped and blinked throughout the chamber, clicking and whirring until they flared to full strength. But the alarms were still sounding, and the red lights were still flashing.

An automated voice spoke in a language Reena didn't know. "Bast?"

The red panda scooted closer to her. "The computer has recognized you as one of the Queen's protectors. Now you will have access."

Reena gaped at him for a moment. "The queen's protectors?" She held up a hand. "Never mind. No time. Tell me later."

The screen flashed and showed several open windows of streaming characters. Mica got to her feet behind Reena and stared.

"It's gibberish," she whispered.

Reena gaped, her mind whirring to keep up. "It's Quantum pseudocode."

"It's what?" Mica clutched her freckled face with both hands. "Is it contagious?"

"It's a programming language Jim taught me." Reena regarded the foreign keyboard on the terminal. "I know the syntax, but I don't know these characters."

Bast slid under her arm and tapped a dial in the corner of the terminal. A screen appeared and began flipping through language options.

"Pick one! Quickly!" He pointed.

Each option the screen displayed was more confusing than the next. Squiggles. Intricate characters. Something vaguely cuneiform based. And then—Latin!

Reena hit the dial, and instantly the characters on the screen changed to something that looked a little more familiar.

"Tenestelian Basic?" Bast looked at her with disgust. "Why do you speak that? It's not even in this galaxy."

"It's close enough." Reena ignored him and focused on the screen and her fingers, adding the lines of code she needed to access the systems that were currently active in the base. "Mica, remind me to thank Jim for forcing me to learn Latin."

Mica grunted in response and chewed on her fingernails.

Heart thumping in her chest, brain whirring through all the possible options and nested statements she'd need to mine for the necessary data, Reena muttered under her breath and kept entering code. Finally, a screen popped open that listed currently active security precautions.

"Got it!" Reena squealed.

She accessed the root commands for the equivalent of the lockdown systems and deactivated them.

Immediately, the alarm cut off mid-warble, and the red lights quit flashing. Reena held her breath. So did Mica. Bast stared at her in shock.

"You did it," he breathed. "How did you do that? I only ever saw the Custodian deactivate the Ikroza's security systems."

Reena sank to the floor and bunched the collar of her shirt in her fist, releasing a shaking breath. "I was guessing really. But it made sense."

Mica hugged her tightly, and they sat still and quiet for a moment. Then, the other systems inside the chamber began to whir and activate. A loud *THUNK* jolted them both back to their feet, clinging to each other.

"What was that?" Mica yelped. "Are we dying?"

Ahead of them, the giant metal bulkhead split in the center and opened, like a curtain being parted. Behind it lay the vast expanse of the night sky, black velvet studded with twinkling stars, and the shimmering atmosphere of the Earth itself.

Reena's mouth hung open. Mica squeaked like a hyperventilating gerbil.

Earth.

Planet Earth.

"Reena?" Mica gasped. "That's Earth."

"Yes."

"If we're looking at Earth that means we're not on Earth."

"Yes."

They both turned to Bast who stood at their feet.

"Bast? Explain!" Reena trembled.

"I told you. This is the Ikroza." He shrugged, his tail flicking back and forth. "This is very bad. Very bad indeed."

"We're in space!" Mica's voice had risen three octaves.

"We are in geosynchronous orbit of Planet Bet-Hadash, yes." Bast gestured to the viewing window where Earth hung like a swirling white, blue, and green gemstone. "And that is not where the Ikroza should be." He gazed out the window. "The Ikroza was stationed on Ebi Inyanga. The moon of Bet-Hadash."

Reena took a long, deep breath. "Bast, what is this?"

The little red panda turned back to them, his expression mournful. "Ebi Inyanga has fallen. That is the only explanation. The Inyanga Bukhosi is no more. The Lunar Empire of the Great Queen Aiyetoro is gone." He shuddered. "How can it be? How?"

Reena lowered herself to the metal floor, and Bast approached her quietly.

"We're not in danger of dying now, I assume?" Reena raised her eyebrows.

"The system is secure, yes." Bast settled at her knees.

"Can you explain what's happening?" Reena asked. "Please?

The visions I saw of my father's sister made no sense."

Bast regarded her with a scowl. "Lady Hanihaweeyo is your father's sister?"

"Yes, Eedo Hani."

"Ah." Bast folded his arms again. "Then your father is Prince Jameilas."

"Prince?" Reena shook herself. "Bast—what are you talking about? My dad isn't a prince."

"If the woman you saw in the vision was your aunt, then your father is Jameilas, the Crown Prince of Arawelo."

Reena pressed shaking fingers into the sides of her head. It was too much information, too many words, and none of it made sense.

Bast tilted his furry head. "The High King of Arawelo had two children, Prince Jameilas and Princess Hanihaweeyo. The Princess was selected as all Inyanga Bukhosi princesses are to serve as the guardian of the Queen Under the Moon. And I am the Khonzi of Inamba Yeziko."

Reena held up her hands. "Stop."

Bast fell silent.

Reena took a moment to breathe. "What is Arawelo?"

Bast's silence continued, his eyes growing wider with every silent moment.

"Is that a bad question?" Mica sat across from them and leaned forward. "I've been wondering too."

"What is Arawelo?" Bast stared at her in horror.

Reena lifted her hands palms up. "That's what I asked you, mister."

"Arawelo is your heritage!" Bast's fur bristled. "Arawelo is your world! Arawelo is your people!"

"Bast, I don't know what that means." Reena set her hands on her knees. "I don't know what Arawelo is or where it is or who it is. What is it?"

Bast pointed upward with one of his paws. "Arawelo is there."

Reena turned her gaze upward and gasped.

"Whoa," Mica whispered.

Above them, engraved on the ceiling tiles, was an intricate carving of the solar system. The Sun, blazing at the center. The silvery flowering moon of Earth, shimmering incandescently as though it were the focal point. The other nine planets in orbit.

"Arawelo is a planet?" Reena blinked.

"Which one?" Mica screwed up her face.

Reena turned her eyes back to Bast. "Are you saying I'm from another planet?"

Bast stared at her, horrified. "How can you not know this?"

"Well maybe because nobody told me?" Reena squeaked. "How can I be from another planet?"

"Your father is the Crown Prince of Arawelo," Bast said slowly, emphatically. "The planet nearest the Sun."

"Mercury?"

Surely the little furry alien creature was wrong. Surely he

had her mixed up with someone else.

Bast scoffed. "That is the Bet-Hadash word for our beautiful world."

"Bet-Hadash?" Mica asked and pointed out the window. "Earth?"

Bast wrinkled his snout. "Earth?" He said the word like it tasted bad. "What a disgusting name."

"Reena," Mica breathed, staring at her, "you're from Mercury. You're from another planet."

"It's a mistake," Reena said. "It's all a mistake."

Bast hissed sharply.

"There is no mistake," he snapped. "The Heart of Arawelo is never mistaken. Your family is the royal family of Arawelo."

Mica lowered herself to a crouch. "Are you okay?"

"I'm an alien, Mica. No, I'm not okay."

"I didn't think so." Mica patted her knee gently. "I wouldn't be okay if I found out I was an alien. But—you're the nicest alien I've ever met."

Reena glanced at her with a dry smile.

"If that helps?" Mica shrugged.

"It kind of does."

A bright smile curled up Mica's face. "You're an alien, Reena. And a princess! That's actually really cool."

Reena smiled back.

Yes, everyone needed a friend like Mica.

"It will feel cool later, I'm sure." Reena shook herself. "But

Dad has some major storytelling to do when I get home." She chewed her lip. "Why didn't he tell me?"

Mica rested her elbows on her knees. "Do you think your mom knows?"

Good question.

A question she didn't know the answer to.

"I've always thought my dad was honest," Reena said softly. "I always trusted him to tell the truth." She gazed down at her hands, which looked awfully like an Earthling's hands unless you knew different. "He could never tell us everything about his work."

"All the top-secret stuff," Mica whispered.

"Yeah. Maybe this is the same." Reena closed her fists. "Maybe he didn't tell us because he couldn't tell us. Or it just wasn't the right time."

Mica nodded. "That sounds like your dad."

Reena smiled. "It does sound like him." She took a steadying breath. "Okay. We'll ask him when we get back to Earth."

"Earth." Mica snickered as she stood and walked to the window to gaze out at the stars. "Bast is right. Bet-Hadash sounds way better."

Bast crawled up in Reena's lap.

"I am sorry, *amiirad*," Bast said. "This was not the revelation I had hoped to provide you with."

"So, you can turn into a giant pink sparkly dragon, huh?"

He smirked again. "Yes, with your help."

"Why me?"

Bast nodded toward the glowing pink jewel on the dash of the computer terminal. "You are the Heart of Arawelo now. We are bonded."

"That's why I could see and hear your thoughts," Reena said.

"Yes. Our bond will grow stronger with time."

"Why were you in my dad's office?" Reena leaned back with her hands spread on the floor. "And why did you hatch out of a rock?"

Bast settled in her lap, blinking up at her. "When those of my race, the Ayasahgala, are mortally wounded, we return to our stone form to heal." His furry eyebrows bunched together above his shining black eyes. "I can only assume that your aunt recovered my *ausara* and gave it to your father until you came of age."

"*Ausara*? The geode? Your egg?"

Bast nodded. "If Ebi Inyanga yet remained, I would know what we were to do, but if it has indeed fallen?" He sighed. "I do not know what our purpose is now. Without the royal family, we have no reason to be. The Dragons of the Diamond Throne exist to protect the Queen Under the Moon, and if she is gone? And her whole family with her?"

Reena patted his head again, and this time he didn't swat her hand away. "Could some of her family have survived?" She bit her lip. "Did she have children?"

"She had many children." Bast smiled almost to himself. "The youngest was the Princess Akeyo, but if even the king has fallen, I cannot imagine she would have survived."

"Reena!"

Reena turned toward Mica's voice. Somehow her friend had wandered into another room within the Ikroza.

"What is it?" Reena got to her feet, carrying Bast with her.

"Come here!"

Bast nodded. "Yes, you should see what your strange little friend has found."

Reena carried Bast into the adjoining chamber. As they entered the lights around the circumference of the room sparked and brightened.

"Whoa," Reena gasped.

A gigantic stone statue of a dragon loomed at the center of the chamber, wings spread, clawed talons outstretched, tooth-filled snout open wide in a silent roar. The spikes adorning its head studded its spine all the way down to its spiked tail.

It had to be forty feet tall. It was bigger than Bast had been in dragon form.

"Incredible," Reena breathed.

"No." Bast hid his face in Reena's shoulder, his voice shaking with grief. "Then it is true."

Reena gazed down at him. "What's wrong?"

"That is not a statue, *amiirad*." Bast gazed mournfully at the dragon. "That is the mighty Khanyiso, our great commander."

Mica poked her head around the side of the dragon's tail. "This is a real dragon?"

"Yes." Bast nodded sadly. "My dearest friend."

Reena approached quietly. "I'm so sorry, Bast. How did this happen?"

Bast didn't respond right away and turned his gaze to the platform where Khanyiso sat. He pointed to the glass containment chambers encircling the statue. The one closest to them was empty.

"Behold."

Mica came around the side of the dragon's knuckle, her hand lingering against its skin between two misshapen scales and peered into the glass container. "It's--a rock."

Reena looked as well. Inside the glass chamber, a large stone about the size of a gallon of milk sparkled in the overhead lights. The skin of the shell seemed iridescent, shifting between blue and green.

Reena caught her breath. "That looks just like your egg. That's—an *ausara*, right?"

"Yes." Bast turned in Reena's arm. "If all these *ausara* are here, it means that all the dragon defenders of the royal family of the moon have fallen." His voice trembled. "This is the Khonzi of Kaiohana." He pointed to the next container, which held an egg that shimmered violet. "That is the Khonzi of Haleine. Beyond it, the Khonzi of Mishnota."

"Wait, these are dragons?" Mica stopped him. "Like you?"

Reena met her eyes. "Bast's kind reverts to an egg form to heal when they're wounded in battle."

"Wow," Mica whispered. "Each one of these stone eggs is a red panda like you? That can turn into a dragon like you?"

"Similar." Bast sniffed. "But, yes, one *ausara* for each of the eight worlds within the Inyanga Bukhosi."

Mica frowned. "Eight worlds? But there are nine planets."

Bast sniffed. "Bet-Hadash never joined the empire. Not in the traditional sense."

Reena slowly walked the perimeter of the room as Bast continued to talk, pointing out the different eggs in the containment chambers and sharing personal details about each occupant. Reena had mostly tuned him out until his voice cut off.

"Where is the Khonzi of Yematenga?" Bast gasped.

He leaped out of her arms and scrambled up onto the platform where the empty glass container shone dully in the lights.

"Yematenga?" Reena asked.

"The Ringed Planet."

"Saturn?"

Bast dismissed her with a wave. "This is most irregular. The Khonzi would only be absent in a situation like this if the Inamba had been chosen, but if Inamba Yamoya has been selected, why isn't she here?"

"Reena!"

Reena tried not to roll her eyes. "What now, Mica?" She stepped into the further darkness at the back of the chamber, and the lights brightened again.

Reena froze mid-step.

Nine glass chambers lined the back wall of the chamber. Within each chamber, except one, stood silver mannequins wearing armor—dragon armor.

Mica pointed with her mouth hanging open. "Look at this! Reena, look!"

The centermost chamber bore an armor of green and blue scales. The armor in the chamber beside it was pink and bronze—the same armor Reena had seen Eedo Hani wearing in her visions. Displayed on the wall behind it hung a bronze and silver bow that shimmered in the lights.

Bast smiled up at her. "Inamba Yeziko." Then he smiled at the armor. "The Heart of Arawelo. The Dragon of Mercury."

"That's me?" Reena whispered.

"Yes," Bast said.

"I get armor?"

"Surely you did not expect to go into battle with nothing but your skin and your little knife tool?" Bast snickered.

"Battle?" Reena stared at him. "Battle with what? With who? I don't know how to fight. I'm a techie computer nerd, not a warrior."

I couldn't even make it as a Peregrine field agent. I'm not a superhero!

With a whirring sound, another alarm began to sound. This one was different than the original security alarm. Less panic-inducing but no less urgent.

"What now?" Mica groaned.

Reena let Bast jump down, and she ran to the computer terminal where a yellow light flashed to the same rhythm of the alarm. On the screen, a message blinked in large Latin characters.

"Pro-pen-quit-us money-toe-um?" Mica sounded out the syllables.

Reena tried not to groan. Kansans could mispronounce anything.

"*Propinquitas Monitionem,*" Reena corrected. "Latin remember? It's a proximity alarm. But for what?" She typed a line of code on the keyboard, and a topographical map of Earth appeared on the screen.

It showed a red dot blinking and began to zoom in on it. The image increased in magnification until it was clear the alert was pointing to Kansas. Wichita specifically.

"Uh-oh," Reena groaned.

"Does that mean what I think it means?" Mica pointed.

Bast turned a grim expression on both of them. "Whatever triggered the alarm is headed directly for your city."

Reena gawked at the screen in horror, the ominous red dot flashing in time with her panicked pulse.

"What is it?" She leaned closer to the screen, as though she could see details in the flashing dot. "Is it a monster? A spaceship? What, Bast?"

Bast scrambled across the computer terminal until he found whatever he was looking for. He poked a few buttons, and a readout popped up on the screen. Reena skimmed the characters. They were in Latin, but they didn't make any sense.

Bast muttered under his breath and pushed a few more buttons until the language on the screen shifted back to the original gibberish it had been.

He sighed. "It's an *usathana.*"

"What?" Mica took Reena's arm. "What is that?"

Bast turned to face them, expression sour. "It's a dragon, if you must know."

"Like you?" Reena looked back at the screen.

"Not like me." Bast shook his head, his ears twitching. "*Usathana* are bred on the dark side of the Moon, the shadowed side. They are brutal and vicious, mindless creatures with no soul or intellect. They only exist for destruction and death."

"Well, that's cheerful." Mica scowled.

"What is it doing in Wichita?" Reena pointed to the screen. "Why did it just show up?"

Bast regarded her calmly. "It has likely been there all the time, my lady." His little white eyebrows drew together over his snout. "I assume our transport here to the Ikroza woke it up."

Reena clutched Mica's hand. "It's after us?"

Bast scooted closer to Reena. "After you, *amiirad*. Do you not yet understand?"

"Me?"

Bast waved a paw at Mica dismissively. "I am certain your little friend is capable, but it is you who matters in this situation. You are the Heart of Arawelo. You must assume the mantle of your aunt and become a Dragon of the Diamond Throne."

"Whoa," Mica whispered. "Fancy."

Reena glared at her. "Mica. Really. Not helping."

"But it's fancy. I wanna be fancy."

Bast snorted and leaped off the computer terminal. "Come with me. Bring the Heart of Arawelo."

He galloped into the other chamber, his bushy tail bouncing as he ran. Snatching the glowing pink jewel off the computer terminal, Reena ran after him, still holding Mica's hand. Bast led them to the dragon armor from before, the pink and bronze one.

Bast stood up beside it with his paws on the glass. "You

must don it, my lady, and we must go into battle."

"Battle?" Reena choked, looking back and forth between the armor behind the glass and Bast at her feet. "I don't do battle. I've never done battle—not like battle-battle. I play chess."

Bast turned to look up at her. "The Heart of Arawelo has already accepted you." He nodded to the shimmering pink gemstone in Reena's hand. "You are the only one who can wield the Dragon Soul of Arawelo, the mighty Ikrele Elivuthayo, and restore the honor of your world and family."

Reena knelt and fisted her hands in the fabric of her shorts. "Bast, listen to me." Her voice shook. "I want to help. I'll do all I can. But I can't fight. I'm not a fighter."

"Reena." Mica sat next to her. "Yes, you are. You're awesome, Reena."

"No, I'm not." Reena's lower lip trembled. "Mica, I don't think I can do this. If I can't be a Peregrine agent, how can I be a superhero?"

Mica fell silent.

Tears burned in Reena's eyes. "I'm not strong enough to be on the field with agents like Barb and Jim. I'm not fast enough or big enough. I'm too small to do anything but program and research and support other people."

Reena's voice caught in her throat as the truth spilled out.

"I'll never be strong enough," she said. "Not like my father. Not like Tay or Cecelia. I'm just me, and I can't fight."

Slowly, Mica reached through the cold air and took her hand, squeezing tightly.

"Reena," Mica said softly, "you fight all the time. You're the strongest person I know." Mica beamed at her, eyes shining. "You never give up, and you're always nice to people—even the people who aren't nice to you. That's the kind of fighting that matters. That's the best kind of fighting there is—fighting to be kind."

Reena sniffled and wiped the tears off her cheeks. "There's a vicious monster dragon headed to attack our city, Mica. I don't think I can kill it with kindness."

Mica raised her eyebrows at Bast. "Call me crazy, but I don't think you have to do anything." She shifted her gaze to the armor behind the glass. "You have armor. And a dragon!" Mica's freckled face became a sun. "You don't have to fight. You can just let them fight for you."

Reena blinked at her best friend, hearing Jim's voice at the back of her mind.

Being the smartest or the strongest isn't all it's cracked up to be. Just be good at what you're good at.

He hadn't been sad when he told her she'd failed the exam; he'd been happy, almost relieved. She'd thought it was what he expected, that she would fail, but Jim never expected her to do anything but succeed.

Mica took Reena's other hand with a reluctant smile. "You can't be good at everything, Reena," Mica shrugged.

"That's what Cecelia said too."

Mica grinned. "Well, since both Cecelia and I said it, it must be true, right?"

Reena wrapped her arms around Mica's neck and held on to her, eyes squeezed shut. She should have told Mica sooner. Mica always had a way of looking at things that dragged the sun out from behind the clouds.

Bast cleared his throat. "Not to interrupt this highly emotional moment," his tone sounded irritated, "but your pale, skinny friend is right."

Reena pulled back from Mica and looked down at him. "I don't have to fight?"

"No," Bast shook his head again. "You must fight. But you needn't use your own strength. That is why you have armor." He pointed to the glassed-in chamber and the bronze-and-pink dragon armor that gazed down at them. "And you needn't battle a dragon—not when you have me. We must work together to bring this threat against your city to an end." Bast hesitated. "But you will need to be present. I cannot promise that you will not be injured." The little furry creature crawled to Reena's knees and stared up into her face. "But I can promise that whatever battle you face, I will face it with you, and my strength will be yours."

Reena squeezed Mica's hand.

She took a long, deep breath. And she held her hand out to Bast, who took it with his paws.

"All right," she said. "Show me what I have to do."

Bast shooed Mica away with his paws, and she giggled and stepped back from Reena's side.

"Take the Heart of Arawelo in your hands." Bast cupped his paws.

Reena stood up and did as he showed her. The pink gem flashed and sparkled with a million points of light inside.

"To bond yourself to the armor, you must speak the pledge," Bast said. "And then the armor will come to you whenever you call it."

Reena nodded. "What's the pledge?"

"Speak your name."

"I, Sareena Ellis—"

Bast nodded in approval and shivered his tail. "Declare your vow to bear the Dragon Soul of Arawelo."

Reena licked her lips. "I, Sareena Ellis, vow to bear the Dragon Soul of Arawelo."

The moment the words left her mouth, the jewel in her hands burst into pink shifting light, filling the entire chamber with rose-colored radiance.

"Pledge your sword to protect."

Reena turned her eyes to the armor and watched as the lights around them pulsed in time with her heartbeat. "I pledge my sword to protect."

"Your heart to serve, your mind to wisdom."

"I pledge my heart to serve." Reena trembled as a wave of heat washed over her skin, "and my mind to wisdom."

"Your life for the Diamond Throne."

Energy spilled out of the pink jewel in her hands, lifting her braids off her shoulders and rippling her clothing in its power. "My life," she whispered, watching the eyes of the Dragon Armor sparkle, "for the Diamond Throne."

"Repeat," Bast said. "*Ade akhululwe—*"

"*Ade akhululwe—*"

"*—okanye afe.*"

"*—okanye afe.*"

The pulsing jewel Reena held erupted in a blaze of fiery light, sweeping up her arms and over her shoulders. Searing heat followed the pink fire, surrounding her completely but not burning her. In the swirling tunnel of fire, Reena felt a sigh of relief in the back of her mind, as though a powerful force had been holding its breath and suddenly released it.

With a blow that felt like thunder, the fire vanished.

Reena stood in place, unmoving, uncertain of what had happened. Her vision felt narrower somehow, as though her eyes were seeing through a filter. Her skin tingled, and the dark chamber was brighter. No, not brighter--a different color?

Reena blinked at Mica, who stood staring at her slack-jawed.

"What?" Reena asked and looked down.

Her stomach flipped.

"Oh."

Her arms and hands were covered in armor.

"Whoa."

She turned to find a reflective surface and gawked at the armored figure she saw.

That's me? I'm wearing armor?

The pink and bronze armor from the glassed-in case covered her from head to toe. She wore the helmet shaped like a dragon's face, a clear glass visor covering her eyes. Scaled armor hung from her shoulders and protected her forearms, her shins, and her hips. A strange fabric patterned with dragon scales protected her skin from the armor itself, but it was cool to the touch, like metal.

"Wow," she whispered.

Bast bounded off the floor and leaped up to her shoulder. "It suits you well, *amiirad*."

"How do you feel?" Mica took a step toward her.

"Weird," Reena said, holding her gloved hands up to examine the metallic not-fabric between her fingers. "Very weird."

"You look epic." Mica grinned.

Reena turned to face Bast who perched on her shoulder plate. "Are you sure about this?"

Bast nodded. "I am. You unbound me from my prison of stone. The Heart of Arawelo accepted you. The Dragon Soul of Arawelo has embraced you." He bowed his furry head to her. "Lady Sareena Ellis, Inamba Yeziko, I am yours to command."

Reena patted him on the top of his head, and this time he didn't swat her away.

"And you're going to help me, right?"

Bast smiled. "Always."

Reena nodded. "Okay."

Bast sat back on her shoulder, blinking at her. Reena looked at Mica, who was still grinning, bouncing excitedly from foot to foot.

"Okay," Reena said again.

"Yes." Bast bowed.

Mica bounced.

Reena raised her eyebrows at the red panda before she remembered he couldn't see her expressions in the helmet. "Bast?"

"Yes, my lady."

"How do we go back to Earth?"

Bast shifted his weight slightly. "You must take us."

Reena sighed. *I was afraid of that.* "Bast, I don't know how to do that."

The red panda rolled his eyes. "Ai-yah. This *is* going to take a lot of work."

eena squeezed her eyes shut as the swirling light wrapped around her and Mica, Bast's fur clenched between her fingers. After a rapid-fire tutorial from Bast on how to use her new armor, Reena felt even more uncertain than before.

But like Jim said, sometimes you had to crash before you could boot up.

"Did we make it?" Mica asked from where she was wrapped around Reena's side.

"I don't know," Reena said.

Slowly, Reena cracked her eye open, peering through her lashes through the clear eye-shield of her helmet to the rippling green grasses of Riverside Park and the rushing brown waters of the Little Arkansas River.

Reena sagged in relief. "We made it."

"We made it?" Mica lifted her head off Reena's shoulder and looked around. "Hey! We made it!" She stepped back and thumped Reena on the arm. "You're going to get the hang of this superhero stuff before you know it."

"Thanks."

Bast leaped off Reena's shoulder and stood in front of her.

"We haven't much time," Bast said. "When the *usathana* arrives, you must take hold of me so that I may transform into my dragon form."

Reena frowned. "You can't do that yourself?"

Bast shook his head. "I need to be in contact with you. As our partnership grows stronger, I will need your help less and less, but I am still weak. For now, I must have your help."

"Show me what to do." Reena held out her arms.

Bast jumped into her grasp, flicking his tail and turning his nose to the sky. "We should seek to get outside the city," Bast said. "This conflict will draw unnecessary attention. And your Bet-Hadash is very different from the one I knew."

"Better?" Mica perked up.

Bast scowled at her. "Bet-Hadash is the refuse dump of the solar system." He sniffed the air. "Seems to me not much has changed."

Mica tilted her head at him. "You're a deeply negative person for someone so cute and cuddly."

Bast scoffed and shooed her away again. "Be gone. Take cover. Conceal your garish hair so the *usathana* does not incinerate you."

"She can't come with us?" Reena startled.

She hadn't expected that. Why couldn't Mica come along?

Bast lifted his grumpy eyebrows at her. "You would bring your pale, skinny, fragile little friend into a dragon battle?

Weaponless? Unarmored?"

Reena hesitated. "Well, when you say it like that, it sounds awful."

A chorus of honking horns and squealing brakes tore through the peaceful afternoon air, and a huge shadow streaked overhead, so fast the movement made the wind shift.

Reena gulped. "Is that it?"

"It is time." Bast turned in her arms. "Take hold of my shoulders."

Reena held him by his little furry shoulders.

"And hang on for your life, my lady."

Reena started to reply with something sarcastic or witty, but all the breath left her lungs as Bast's narrow little shoulders went rigid under her fingers. The little red panda roared, a hollow, echoing cacophony of sounds that were far too big to come from an animal so small. Under her hands, the little animal shifted and grew, expanding and enlarging. His fur turned to dragon scales, and his stripes faded to sparkling iridescent skin. Reena choked on a gasp of alarm as his rapid growth catapulted her into the air until she found herself astride his back, clinging to the spikes that studded his spine.

Full size now, twenty feet tall at the shoulder, Bast swung his giraffe-like neck and bellowed a thunderous roar. He snapped his massive wings open and jumped, catching the wind as it built under him and soared into the sky.

Reena clung to his back, gasping for air until she realized that holding on to him felt as natural as clinging to the handlebars of her scooter. Her armored fingers had more strength in them than before. The wind didn't throw her around as violently as before, and the weight of exhaustion she'd felt was gone.

Before them lay the expanse of the bluest summer skies. Puffy clouds danced in the high-altitude winds, and the metropolitan footprint of the city spread out beneath them like one of her grandmother's quilts.

Amazing.

"Wow!"

Bast banked on a thermal and cast a look backward at her, his face so different now than it had been in his much-smaller form. His face was different, but the constant sour expression remained.

Incredible. She held tight to one of his spikes.

Did you not trust me, my lady? Bast's voice resonated in her mind.

Reena froze and stopped breathing. *Bast?*

We are linked in our minds, my lady. In this form I cannot speak, but you can hear me. He glanced back at her again. *Be sure you do not release me. I draw the power to remain in this form from your armor.*

Reena frowned. *I didn't have my armor the first time.*

I was forced to draw energy directly from you, my lady. Bast turned his attention to the dark shadow in front of them. *I drained you of your energy, which is why you could not remain conscious. We will not do that again.*

Reena bent closer to his back and held tighter to his spines.

What do you need me to do?

Bast growled deep in his chest, the strength of it vibrating through his whole body and into Reena's as she clung to him.

Hold tight to me and do not let go. He flapped his wings. *We will make short work of this enemy.*

Reena nodded and held her breath as Bast approached the monstrous figure before them. The closer they got, the bigger it got. Reena swallowed hard at the size of the other dragon.

Its lower jaw protruded past its upper lip, jagged teeth as tall as grown men. Crooked, misshapen horns twisted away from its square-shaped skull, and its deep-set eyes glowed a sickly color between yellow and green.

It has only one directive, Bast's voice resonated in Reena's mind. *To destroy. It will wreak havoc on your city if we do not stop it here.*

A series of horrific images flickered in Reena's mind. Memories, but not hers. Bast's memories of facing black dragons like this one on other battlefields, beneath unfamiliar skies.

"But why?" Reena whispered. "Why now?"

Bast shivered beneath her. *Because I am awake. And so are you.*

The *usathana* sensed them coming and whirled in midair, opening a giant maw full of more teeth than Reena had ever seen as it screamed at them. Bast didn't even hesitate; he rushed right up on the giant black dragon and loosed a stream of fire out of his mouth.

Reena cried out in shock as the raging stream of flame and

light erupted out of Bast's mouth and blasted the black dragon sideways in the sky.

"You can breathe fire?" Reena screamed.

Of course I can breathe fire. Even his telepathic voice sounded perturbed.

Reena held on as he spun around in the air and bore down on the black dragon as it tumbled through the clouds. Reena peered around Bast's flapping wing joint, and as she narrowed her eyes, her helmet flared to life.

The eye-coverings flashed, and a digital readout flashed the details of everything that was happening around her. Wind speed. Velocity. Mass of the planet. Gravitational force. Magnification factor.

Whoa, whoa, whoa.

Bast staggered in the air. *What? What?*

Not you, no, my helmet is doing something.

Bast uttered an annoyed sound. *Stop thinking.*

Reena laughed. Was he serious? Stop thinking? That was impossible. But that probably wouldn't help Bast at the moment.

The black dragon pulled out of its flailing dive, flapping its monstrous skeletal wings and climbing higher into the atmosphere.

Closer now and armed with a helmet that could magnify what she was seeing, Reena zoomed in on the creature. The beast had talons as long as a car's bumper and as wide as a sedan. Its scaled black skin was cracked and broken like it had been dried out or crusted over repeatedly, and the horns and spines all over its body seemed almost rusty in color. As though it had been horribly wounded and not allowed to heal before infection set in. The dragon had no eyes to speak of, and its square jaw hung open, dripping with something wet.

And astride the dragon's back was a person.

Bast! The dragon has a rider! Reena focused on the figure clinging to the black dragon's back.

Impossible.

Reena rolled her eyes. *I'm looking right at him.*

Bast huffed and beat his wings harder against the wind until he'd overtaken the *usathana.* Bast sailed closer and roared at the other dragon until it spun and opened its mouth wide to spew something foul and viscous through the air at them.

Bast yelped and closed his wings, so they dropped out of the path of the liquid. Reena clung to his back and screamed. He came to an abrupt stop as he snapped his wings open and sailed back toward the top of the sky.

I was wrong. Bast's voice sounded shaken. *This is not an* usathana. *It is much worse.*

Reena pried her eyes open. *How can it be worse?*

An usathana *is easy to defeat.* Bast snapped his tail against the winds. *This is a* khohlakele, *a hybrid. It is bonded to the* nanto *on its back much like you are bonded to me.*

"Great. And it's even harder to pronounce."

We must get it out of the sky. Bast flapped harder and sailed through the clouds like a bullet. *You must tell me how close we are to the ground.*

"I have to do what?"

Bast lunged for the other dragon and sank his massive fangs into its neck. The black dragon screamed and thrashed and flailed.

Astride its back, the *nanto* clung to the black dragon, its silver armor flashing in the sunlight. Reena narrowed her eyes at it, and her helmet visor zeroed-in on the *nanto* and zoomed.

Its robotic face stared at her lifelessly, gray LED lights flashing in its mechanical face.

"It's a robot?" Reena gasped.

Bast dug his claws into the black dragon's wing joints and ripped.

They dropped out of the sky.

Reena shrieked as the wind buffeted her against his spikes, tumbling end over end through the winds and clouds, spinning out of control.

The ground, my lady! Where is the ground?

Sobbing in terror, Reena peeled her eyes open to peer through the visor of her helmet. The grass of Riverside Park waved like velvet beneath them. Eight hundred feet. Seven hundred. Six.

Coming up fast!

Below them, Mica ran for cover. She hadn't taken shelter earlier like Bast had ordered, but at least she had the sense to do it now.

At one hundred feet, tell me!

Reena clung to his spikes and tried not to panic as the black dragon wrestled and roared against Bast's hold.

Four hundred.

Three.

Two.

Now, Bast!!

With a surge of energy and a roar of effort, Bast dug his claws into the black dragon's skin, ripping its wings and dislocating its shoulders and using the leverage to launch himself into the sky.

The black dragon smashed into the grass of Riverside Park with a choked-sounding shriek, splaying sideways and tearing up the lawn as it skidded to a stop along Nims Avenue.

"We got him!" Reena screamed.

That was easier than I thought.

She eyed the traffic zooming away from the downed dragon and the scattered crowds of people fleeing in terror across the park.

Bast cornered in the air. *It's not done yet.* He held his wings in tightly, turning himself into a needle in the air as he shot toward the struggling dragon on the ground.

Bast, you have to slow down! I won't be able—

Bast hit the downed dragon with the power of a freight train, driving it deeper into the dirt. Reena's armored fingers slipped off the scales of his neck, the impact flinging her through the air. She smashed into the grass and dirt with enough force to empty her lungs, and the world tilted around her madly as her body rolled end over end.

Gasping with panic, she flailed to slow her momentum, and

she tumbled to a halt in a pile of torn-up turf and clumps of mud.

The *khohlakele* screeched in rage behind her. She lifted her head and watched the giant dragon pulling itself out of the crater, its rider still holding on to its back.

Bast was gone.

"Bast?" Reena clambered to her feet. "Bast, where are you?"

Movement at the dragon's foot drew her attention to Bast's furry little body, not moving and limp.

I let go.

Bast couldn't maintain his dragon form without holding contact with Reena. If they had any chance of defeating the black dragon, she had to touch Bast again.

I have to get to Bast!

She stumbled forward and stopped short as the black dragon spit another mouthful of that foul, horrible liquid out of its mouth. The toxic drool touched the grass and wilted it, turning it the color of a bruise.

"Acid? It spits acid?" Reena groaned and clutched her forearm, which had begun to ache as soon as she'd stood up. "Not fair."

On the black dragon's back, the *nanto* straightened and glared down at her. Again, her helmet magnified her sight. The rider wore chrome armor covered in crisscrossing chains, but as far as Reena could see he had no helmet. And not much of a face.

It really is a robot. I don't think it's alive.

"Reena!"

Reena spun around as Mica waved at her from the Kansas Wildlife Exhibit building. Even from this distance, Reena could hear the birds and other native animals inside the display screeching in fear.

"Oh, that's probably bad."

The black dragon lurched toward her, its footsteps shaking the ground.

Reena backed away slowly, her enhanced vision zeroing in on Bast's limp body. The black dragon didn't even see him and stepped right over him.

The horrible beast let its lower jaw drop open, showing off an improbably number of teeth, boiling acid dribbling onto the grass.

Mica. Reena gasped and clutched her side. *It's going to shoot acid at Mica.*

What did she do? What could she do?

She turned and studied the roundabout at the edge of the park that connected Stackman Drive and Nims Avenue. Two decorative stone arches stood on either side of Nims.

The dragon inhaled, its breath rattling ominously in its scaled chest.

"Mica, run!"

Mica stopped waving, her eyes wide, and she spun on her heels and dashed as fast as she could as the dragon spewed a mouthful of toxic acid onto the driveway of the Kansas Wildlife Exhibit. A pick-up truck parked in the driveway hissed and sparked as the venom melted it, tires popping and smoking as they disintegrated.

Tornado sirens wailed around them. Apparently, the city officials had finally noticed the mess they were making.

The warbling noise made the black dragon stop and sniff the air in surprise.

Hardly a tornado. Reena scoffed to herself. *And I don't think hiding in a basement is going to help in this instance.*

The distant call of fire trucks and police cruisers blared through the city, getting closer and closer.

We have to deal with this before they arrive. They're no match for a dragon. Reena clenched her fists. *I'm no match for it either. But I've got to do something!*

On the back of the dragon, the *nanto* spun its head completely around.

Yeah. Definitely a robot. Check.

Its flashing eyes fixed on her, and the dragon shifted its weight toward her.

Reena pressed her hand into her chest plate.

"They're bonded," she whispered and glanced toward Bast's limp body. "They're bonded like Bast and I are bonded." Her heart raced. "If I get the *nanto* off the dragon's back, maybe it'll shrink like Bast did?"

It was an insane theory with no evidence. Just because it had worked that way for her and Bast didn't guarantee that the nanto and the black dragon would be the same. But she didn't have time to experiment.

And sometimes your best guess is all you've got. She smiled to herself, remembering Jim's advice from their last catastrophic experiment. *It wasn't exactly the best advice, but he wasn't exactly wrong either.*

The menacing dragon closed the distance between them, venom steaming in its massive mouth.

"Oh, this is a bad idea." Reena groaned.

Reena darted away from the black dragon and ran directly toward the eastern stone arch. The *nanto* nudged the dragon after her, and it followed.

The armor must have been enhancing her physical ability, Reena realized as she ran. After hitting the ground as hard as she had, she should have been out of commission.

She raced to the arch and bolted through it.

The dragon followed her without even hesitating, and the arch collapsed around the dragon's shoulders as it tried to claw its way after her. But the *nanto* held on.

"Good to know you're not very smart!" Reena shouted at it and ran across Nims Avenue to the second arch. "And you're ugly too!"

The dragon flailed and thrashed, trying to escape the collapsed framework of the stone arch and spewed venom all over the ground and its own legs in the process.

Scales and skin steaming and melting, the dragon screamed and charged after her with murder flashing in its eyes.

Reena ran through the second arch.

And the dragon followed.

Definitely not smart.

The second arch collapsed around it, the remnants of the first arch still strangling it. The falling stones knocked the *nanto* sideways, but it didn't fall.

The dragon clawed up the earth and the asphalt, thrashing its tail because its neck was weighed down by the stone archway.

The *nanto* stood up from its mount between the dragon's shoulders.

If only I had something to throw. Reena scanned the area and couldn't find anything.

The dragon began to calm down and narrowed its eyes at her, opening its mouth.

"Reena!"

Reena glanced over her shoulder to see Mica awkwardly galloping toward her, dragging a dark green trash dumpster, its plastic wheels rattling and rumbling on the concrete.

"What am I going to do with that?" Reena flapped her arms.

"Throw it!" Mica yanked the dumpster along behind her. "It smells terrible!"

Reena paused and looked at her arms. If the armor had enhanced her ability to run, maybe it made her stronger all the way around. And she'd wanted something to throw.

Mica shoved the dumpster toward her, and Reena grabbed it.

The *nanto* regained its seat.

I won't get another chance.

And, wow, Mica was right. The dumpster smelled awful.

"Oh, this is such a bad idea." Reena clutched the handles on the dumpster and spun in a tight circle, hurling the plastic trash container through the air with more strength than she'd ever had.

Thank you magic, dragon armor.

The smelly dumpster bin smashed into the *nanto* and knocked it off the dragon's back, spilling a waterfall of rotten food, paper plates, and old candy bar wrappers as it did so.

The *nanto* shrieked metallically as it tumbled off the side of the dragon and landed in a puddle of the dragon's own venom.

The giant menacing dragon shrank and shrank until it was nothing more than a little salamander thrashing in the dirt.

Staring in disbelief, Reena approached the little lizard cautiously. The once-mighty beast kicked up the dust with its little legs and its little tail, helpless and small, as though it had never been giant enough to wreck a city park.

She stood over it, blinking at it until Mica joined her.

"Is that the dragon?"

"Yeah."

"Do we touch it?"

"I don't know."

"What do we do now?"

Reena laughed. "I have no idea, Mica."

Across from them, the *nanto* slowly decomposed in the puddle of venom, spewing sparks and buzzing like a dying radio.

Slowly, Reena approached it, holding Mica behind her. The *nanto* seized and jerked, its burned and melted gears falling apart.

Its robotic face remained locked in a rigid stare, gleaming chrome features lifeless and expressionless, but its glowing eyes flared red.

"*Ukufa*," it droned mechanically, "*kuza*."

With a hiss and a spark, its systems shut down. The moment it deactivated, it disintegrated, turning to ash and blowing away.

"Whoa," Mica whispered.

Reena gasped for breath as the adrenaline caught up with her. Her helmet felt awfully tight suddenly.

"That was amazing," Mica said. "And crazy and nuts and wild and—oh man, really stinky." She waved her hand in front of her face.

Reena agreed with a grunt. Whatever had been in that trash dumpster really stunk up the place.

"Where's Bast?" Mica asked.

"Bast!" Reena spun quickly and ran to where Bast lay. "Bast?" She knelt beside him. "Bast, are you all right?"

Bast snarled at her and blinked his eyes. "I told you not to let go."

"Well, I told you to slow down." Reena heaved a sigh of relief.

Bast sat up and gazed at the torn-up turf and the ash pile that was blowing in the wind. He nodded and flicked his ears.

"You did well, my lady. And all on your own." He smirked

at her. "And you said you're not a fighter."

The wail of an emergency siren pierced the air.

"Uh-oh," Mica said, standing up.

"Yeah, I'm sure the whole city saw it." Reena lifted Bast into her arms. "We need to get out of here."

"What happened to the big bad dragon?" Mica asked.

"Without the *nanto* it's harmless." Bast curled around Reena's shoulders. "Quickly. We must get out of sight. I will teach you how to remove your armor, and then we must get somewhere safe." He sniffed the air. "And then both of you need to clean yourselves. You smell awful."

Mica puffed out her chest. "We beat the bad guys with a trash dumpster."

Bast glared at her. "How very Bet-Hadash of you."

Reena turned to Mica. "We could go home."

Mica smiled. "If you're going home, I'm coming with you." She giggled. "I can't wait to see your sister's face when you tell her you're a superhero."

Reena grunted as she and Mica ran for the end of the park, avoiding the section of grass the dragon venom had melted.

My sister's face? Reena winced to herself. *What about Dad? And Mom? How am I going to explain this to them? I may be a superhero, but I just wrecked Riverside Park. Somehow, I don't think they're going to be thrilled.*

10

Reena swallowed the urge to yawn as the city bus's brakes squealed to a stop on Second Street. Bast, who had curled around her neck like a scarf, snored peacefully and hadn't budged since she and Mica had boarded at Riverside Park.

Mica hadn't said a word, but the girl was vibrating with latent energy. If she didn't get to express herself soon, she would probably spontaneously combust.

Reena stood as soon as the bus stopped moving and walked to the exit door with Mica at her heels. Everyone on the bus was buried in their own projects. Some stared at phone screens. Others read books. None of them noticed a little teenage girl with an alien red panda draped across her shoulders.

Maybe fewer people had noticed the dragon battle than Reena had thought.

Mica stood at her side as the bus door closed, and they watched it lumber down Second Street with its lights flashing. Mica turned to look at her.

Here we go.

"Reena, you're a superhero!" Mica squealed.

"Yes, Mica, apparently I am." Reena gathered Bast from around her neck and cradled his limp body in her arms.

Mica bounced beside her. "I'm sorry, I'm sorry, that was just so cool! The evil black dragon was all like RAWR-rahr-RAWR and you were all shiny and pink and sparkly like Take-That-Foul-Beast! Wham!" Mica reenacted the moments of the airborne battle as best she could without wings or a tail. "That has to be the coolest thing I've ever seen in my life!"

Reena sighed.

"Why aren't you excited?" Mica grabbed her arm. "Reena, we went to space! You're an alien princess with a dragon sidekick!"

Reena glanced at her and couldn't stop a smile. "It is pretty cool, isn't it?"

"Yeah." Mica laughed, beaming for a moment until her face fell. "Unless—are you hurt?"

Reena blinked.

"You've been so quiet. I didn't think. Are you okay? Did you get hurt?" Mica pressed closer to her as they walked up the sidewalk.

"No, Mica, I'm okay. A few bumps and bruises, and I'm just—really tired." Reena rubbed her gritty-feeling eyes. "I just want to go home and talk to my dad and see if he can make sense out of any of this wild, crazy stuff."

She smiled as the house came into view, but she stopped short in sight of the garage. "Uh oh."

"Uh oh, what?" Mica stopped with her.

"Dad's home." Reena nodded to the black metallic Dodge Charger parked in the garage.

"He was out with Cecelia today, wasn't he?" Mica fell into step with Reena as they walked up the driveway together.

"Yeah, they went to Yoder for her birthday." Reena adjusted her hold on Bast. "I don't know, Mica. This might get really ugly."

"Hey." Mica took her arm. "I'm with you. And it's not like I don't already know all your family secrets."

Reena scoffed. "True."

"And you just beat a dragon." Mica nodded somberly. "You can handle your dad."

Reena chuckled. "The moment I think my dad is less scary than a dragon, I'm in trouble."

She scaled the steps into the kitchen hesitantly and cracked the door open. Raised voices from inside the house made her stomach turn over.

Yeah. Not good.

Her father rarely raised his voice. He didn't need to. He had a magical ability to force a confession out of any of his three children with a simple raised eyebrow. Strange, because her mother possessed the ability as well.

Reena had often considered writing a thesis on it, but Jim told her it was just parent skills, since his mother had been able to do it too.

Mica crept into the kitchen behind her, and they approached the family living room together. Slowly, Reena handed Bast over to

Mica, who cradled him with a silent squeal of joy. Bast snored away, his tail twitching happily.

"Cecelia, you must tell us the truth."

Reena paused.

Auntie Kay?

What was Auntie Kay doing here? Auntie Kay hadn't been planning to come over for another week or so. Actually, hadn't she been on a trip to Japan? Had she come back?

Reena angled her position so she could see into the living room.

Cecelia sat on the sofa, arms crossed and face screwed up in an expression of anger. Gone was the cheerful, jovial teenager who'd left that morning looking forward to pie. Now Cecelia was mad. Her shining hair had been swept up on top of her head in a wild bun, and the whole style shook every time she opened her mouth.

"I don't know what you're talking about," Cecelia said. "Either of you!"

Auntie Kay stood at the center of the living room. She wore a vibrant yellow and black patterned business dress, the matching blazer draped over the back of an upholstered chair. Her dark hair, streaked with silver, hung down around her shoulders.

Her father's oldest friend, Kay had come to America with the Ellis family from Somalia decades earlier.

Mica pointed to her and looked at Reena with a question in her eyes. Reena shrugged.

Why is Auntie Kay here? That makes no sense.

Jasper Ellis heaved a heavy sigh from where he sat on the sofa across from his eldest daughter. His khakis and collared shirt looked rumpled, as though he'd been crawling around in a tight space and had only just emerged.

"Cecelia," he spoke slowly and precisely, "it could only have been you."

Cecelia turned away from him, nose in the air. "Well, it had to be someone else, because I didn't do it. I never touched your stupid geode."

Reena gulped.

Oh, this just got worse.

Cecelia was taking the blame for what Reena had done. Probably for what Hermes had done to the house too.

Jasper ran his hands over his face for a moment before he stood and knelt in front of Cecelia. "I understand why you're upset, Cece." He set his hand on her knee. "But I do not understand why you are lying."

Reena sagged against the wall and squeezed her eyes shut. She had to intervene now before the situation got even more complicated. She had so many questions, but letting her sister take the heat for something she hadn't done wasn't right.

Reena gestured to Mica to wait, and Mica lifted her arms where Bast was still snoring. And Reena stepped into the living room.

"Dad?"

Jasper scowled at her. "Sareena, not now." He pointed to the stairwell.

"Dad, Cece didn't do it."

Her father's laser-eyes focused on her. Auntie Kay turned to her with a skeptical face.

"Cecelia didn't do what, Sareena?" Auntie Kay folded her arms, her heavy accent growing stronger with every word.

Reena took a deep breath. "I took the stone."

Her father blinked at her in surprise. "You did?" He stood and faced her.

"You did?" Cecelia gawked at her and pointed. "Have you been upstairs this whole time? Listening to me take your punishment?"

"No." Reena held up her hands.

Cecelia stood up, face set in fury and fists clenched at her sides. "So, you steal his stupid rock, you let Hermes tear the whole house apart, and I get the lecture about it?" Cecelia glared at her father. "I know she's your favorite, but that's not fair, Dad."

"Enough, Cecelia." Jasper held up his hand, but he stopped before he could continue as his cell phone rang. "Of course." He checked the screen. "It's the office. Cecelia, sit down. Sareena, sit down. You two will sit and be silent until I am finished."

He didn't wait for them to agree. He just answered his phone gruffly, "Ellis," and walked out of the room.

Cecelia flared her nostrils and sat down with a huff, not looking at anyone. Reena quietly hurried to a chair and sat, holding a pillow and glancing over her shoulder to where Mica was still hiding in the kitchen.

Auntie Kay stepped in front of her, eyes narrowed.

"Sareena," she began in her rich-toned voice, "you're acting strangely."

Reena pressed her lips together.

"Very strangely."

Auntie Kay wasn't exactly a mind-reader, but she was the closest thing to one that Reena had ever met.

A startled exclamation from the front bedroom drew her attention as Jasper's voice raised again. In his office with the door shut, Reena couldn't make out what he was saying, but he sounded upset.

He knows. She shut her eyes. *Someone in his office saw the whole thing, and now he knows.*

The door to the front bedroom flung open, and he stormed back into the living room.

"Akeyo," he strode directly to Auntie Kay, "the worst has happened. Two dragons were spotted downtown engaged in battle over Riverside Park."

Reena planted her face into the pillow in her lap.

"Dragons?" Cecelia yelped.

"Impossible." Auntie Kay's face twisted. "Impossible, Jasper. It cannot be. And even if it were, it cannot be the *khonzi*. It couldn't transform without bonding to an *agnimitra*."

Auntie Kay's voice drifted away as she set her hand on

Jasper's arm.

"Oh, Jasper." She turned her fierce gaze toward Reena, her eyes going wide. "Oh, my friend, I believe I was wrong."

Jasper scowled. "Wrong about what, Akeyo?"

Auntie Kay approached Reena. "Sareena, you took your father's geode? The stone from his office?"

"Sort of." Reena nodded once.

"Sort of?" Auntie Kay arched her shapely eyebrows. "Explain *sort of*, Sareena."

"It fell off the desk." Reena squirmed. "And I picked it up, and it—hatched."

Her words fell like thunder in the room, shocked silence following.

"It hatched?" Cecelia gasped.

Jasper and Auntie Kay gawked at her with expressions of muted horror.

"You?" Jasper's voice shook.

Reena couldn't hold his gaze. She tore her eyes away and looked toward where Mica was hiding. "You might as well come out, Mica."

"Okay!"

"Mica?" Jasper straightened in surprise.

"Of course, Michaela is involved." Auntie Kay rolled her eyes. "Where one is, there's the other." But she stopped short when Mica stepped into view with Bast lounging in her arms, snoring loudly.

Jasper stared along with her.

"Hi," Mica said weakly with an awkward smile.

Cecelia stood up from the couch, pointing at Bast. "What is that?"

"Well, his name is Bast." Mica lifted him slightly. "He's cute and cuddly and has a really bad attitude. And he doesn't have a lot of helpful information to share. Just saying."

Both the adults in the room stared at Mica and Bast with their mouths open.

"Did you take that from the zoo?" Cecelia set her hands on her hips. "Where did you find that? Is it alive? Why is it pink?"

Reena twisted her fingers together. "He was in the geode. He hatched out of it."

Cecelia looked from Bast to Reena to her father. "Dad? This is messed up."

Jasper's gaze shifted to Auntie Kay. He held his hands palm up, and Auntie Kay shrugged, her expression flabbergasted.

Reena watched their faces.

Shocked.

They were totally caught off guard. In all her life, she'd never seen her father look like that, and she'd certainly never seen Auntie Kay look that way either.

As though she feared any sudden movement would make Bast disappear, Auntie Kay turned to face Reena. "You touched the stone?"

"Last night," Reena said. "It fell last night, and I put it back on the desk. And then it fell again this morning, and he hatched when I picked it up."

The woman glanced toward the sleeping red panda and back to Reena. "Did he give it to you?" Auntie Kay's eyes tightened at the corners, the way they did when she had to talk to someone on the telephone.

"Give what to me?" Reena asked.

"If he gave it to you, then you know what I am asking." Auntie Kay set her jaw.

She wants to know if Bast gave me the Heart of Arawelo.

Slowly, Reena reached into the pocket of her shorts and pulled out the burning, sparkling pink jewel.

Her father whispered a Somali prayer, and Auntie Kay staggered as though something heavy had been laid across her shoulders.

"The Heart of Arawelo," Auntie Kay lowered her head, her eyes misting. "So, it is true. The Lord Bast has chosen you."

Reena trembled. "I'm sorry." She looked at her father. "I didn't know what was going to happen. If I had known, I'd just have left the stone on the floor."

Jasper stepped toward her and enfolded her in his arms, he mumbled something in Somali in her ear, and Reena buried her face in his chest. For a solitary moment, everything was all right.

"Forgive me, Jasper." Auntie Kay's voice sounded thick and heavy with emotion. "I was wrong."

"We were both wrong." Jasper's tone was rough, low. He

was upset, but not at Reena.

Slowly, Reena pulled back and looked up into her father's face and then at Auntie Kay. On the couch, Cecelia's eyebrows were drawn together, and her eyes were full of worry.

"It should have been Cecelia," Auntie Kay said. "Every piece of data I have researched always indicated the eldest daughter would be the *agnimitra*."

"You guys aren't saying real words." Cecelia huffed from the couch and lifted her nose.

Jasper regarded her with a sheepish smile. "Then I owe you an apology."

"You do. Both of you do. Several apologies." Cecelia looked away from him.

Still holding Reena, Jasper turned to look at his older daughter. "Cecelia, I am sorry to have not believed you. You did nothing wrong."

Cecelia flopped back on the couch cushions.

Jasper lifted his eyebrows at her. "Will you forgive me?"

"Yes, Dad, I forgive you." Cecelia kept her eyes narrowed. "I might even forgive the little punk you're snuggling with too."

Reena stuck her tongue out at her.

Jasper set her back and looked into her face. "And the dragons? Battling over the city?"

"Yeah, I guess we made a mess." Reena winced.

"Dragons?" Cecelia gasped. "Like actual dragons?"

"You donned the armor?" Jasper whispered. "The Inamba

Yeziko?"

Reena nodded, breathlessly.

"And the dragon you battled?"

"Bast called it a *khohlakele*."

Auntie Kay's eyes bugged out, and she hissed a Xhosa phrase Reena had never learned.

Jasper laughed without humor, the wrinkles in the corners of his eyes straining. "Sareena, must you always be an overachiever?"

Auntie Kay set her hand on Jasper's shoulder. "There are many stories to tell and much to discuss. But right now, we must go. There is a special place—a hidden place—and I need that gem to unlock it."

"The Ikroza?" Reena sat up.

For the second time that day, both her father and her aunt gawked at her in wordless shock.

"Yeah, been there, done that." Mica shrugged, coming to stand next to Reena. "It's been a day."

Jasper was praying out loud again as he sank into a chair and set his head in his hands. Cecelia stared in shocked silence, clutching a couch pillow in her lap.

"How did you find the Ikroza?" Auntie Kay blinked repeatedly like something was stuck in her eyes.

"Bast took us." Reena nodded to the snoring red panda.

"How did you survive?" Jasper lifted his head, muscle ticking at the back of his jaw. "That is the question. The Ikroza's security systems will kill anyone who enters without authorization."

Mica and Reena glanced at each other and shrugged.

"Well, we were able to get the computer systems running." Reena bit her lower lip. "And from there, I kind of just winged it."

"You winged it?" Auntie Kay's eyes were like saucers.

"Yeah, that makes it sound really irresponsible, doesn't it?"

In Mica's arms, Bast shifted and stretched out, yawning enormously. He sighed and turned to look around the room and paused, big eyes widening.

"Oh." Bast blinked. "What an unexpected sight to awaken to."

Behind Jasper, Cecelia stared. "Did it just talk?"

"Hush, Cece."

"Dad, that zoo animal just talked."

Bast crawled up Mica's arm and leaped down to the floor, sitting on his haunches and staring up at Auntie Kay with wonder on his furry face. Auntie Kay regarded him in regal silence.

They know each other. Reena held her breath. *I don't know how they know each other, but they do.*

"Your Majesty," he whispered in awe, bowing his head until his ears nearly brushed the floor. "When last I saw you, you were but a child. But now, you look so much like your mother."

Reena stiffened. *Auntie Kay's mother?* She held her breath. *Bast said the Queen Under the Moon had a daughter—named Akeyo. Is it Auntie Kay?*

Auntie Kay shut her eyes and sank into a nearby chair, running her hands over her face. When she sat up again, she was smiling, tears in her eyes.

"Hello, Lord Bast." She nodded. "It has been many years."

Bast sat up and glanced at Jasper.

"Yes," Bast said. "Hello, Prince Jameilas." Bast smirked. "Though I hear you have traded the name your great father gave you for something quite Hadashi."

Jasper's expression hardened. "Lord Bast." He nodded shortly. "Much has happened since you slept."

Reena stared at the little red panda.

She'd already accepted it wasn't a normal red panda. It wasn't even a normal dragon. It was a pink-red-panda-dragon-thing. And that in and of itself was impressive, but her father spoke to it with respect? Even reverence? And so did Auntie Kay?

It was just another reminder of how little Reena actually understood.

On the couch, Cecelia ran her hands over her hair in distress. They were going to have to talk for a long time to sort all of this out.

Jasper stepped forward and took Reena's shoulders in his hands. He bent down and kissed her forehead with closed eyes, his expression the strangest mix of pride and dread Reena had ever read on his face. He hadn't looked like that since she'd shown him her results from the Peregrine Academy entrance exams.

Proud.

But terrified.

"There is much to discuss," Auntie Kay said softly. "You girls have had a long day. Michaela, I suggest you go home."

Mica stiffened a bit in surprise at the dismissal, but she only smiled in return. "Sure. Okay. I can do that."

Cecelia slid off the couch. "I volunteer. Talking pink pandas, space princesses, and words I don't know—it's too much." She looked at Mica. "I'll drive you home and maybe you can tell me what my crazy sister was doing all day."

Mica glanced at Reena, and Reena nodded at her.

Mica grinned and ran after Cecelia. They'd meet up later to talk about whatever Auntie Kay had to say that she didn't want to share.

After all, Mica already knew everything, and Reena had no intention of leaving her out of the loop—no matter what Auntie Kay thought.

Reena took a long sip of the lukewarm tea her father had made for her. It had been piping hot when he'd brought it to her, but after she'd finished with her story, it had stopped steaming.

She told them everything. Bast and Hermes' great battle in the house. The wild trek to Epic Center. Mica's horrifying fall, and Bast's first dragon transformation, along with all the visions she'd seen. The Ikroza. The armor. The *khohlakele* and the *nanto* and the smelly trash dumpster that stopped them both.

Jasper hadn't spoken at all. Neither had Auntie Kay.

Finally, when she had finished, the two adults looked at each other in dread and dismay.

"Extraordinary," Auntie Kay murmured and sat back in her chair.

"You could have been killed." Jasper ran his hands into his hair. "Sareena, you will turn my hair gray."

Reena held his hand. "Is it true, Dad? Are we actually alien royalty?"

He squeezed. "Yes. My father, your grandfather, was the King of the planet Mercury."

"Arawelo?" Reena smirked.

"Arawelo." He bowed his head with a smile. "I was destined for the throne, and my sister Hani was selected to protect the royal family of the empire, the Inyanga Bukhosi."

"The Queen Under the Moon." Reena glanced at Auntie Kay. "That's what Bast said."

"Queen Aiyetoro." Auntie Kay looked down at her hands. "My mother."

Reena sat up. "It's you? You're the one I vowed to protect with my life?"

Jasper shifted with an uncomfortable sigh. "Yes, you would have done that, wouldn't you?"

Reena held up the pink jewel. "I had to make an epic vow, Dad. It was like something out of a comic book or a fantasy movie."

Auntie Kay chuckled. "You have been so brave, Sareena. I knew you were strong, but you have shown yourself so much stronger than I expected." She shut her eyes. "I am sorry we did not know it was you. We would have made many different decisions had we known."

Auntie Kay's eyes shone in the sunlight of the living room, sparkling with unshed tears. Auntie Kay wouldn't cry, of course. She never cried.

Reena slid off the couch and flung her arms around Auntie Kay's neck, holding her tightly.

"I love you, Auntie Kay," she said. "Stop apologizing. You both did the best you could." She looked to her dad. "Do you know why Bast chose me instead of Cecelia?"

Auntie Kay and Jasper traded another look.

"No," Auntie Kay said. "I have no answers for you, Sareena. There is much about the Dragon Armors I do not understand. Your father and I were very young when my mother's kingdom fell. And as a princess, I wasn't taught the operations of the Ikroza; just that it housed my defenders."

"We had some materials," Jasper said. "But apparently our interpretation of those materials is incorrect." He cupped the back of Reena's head. "And speaking of the Ikroza, we ought to check it."

"Yes." Auntie Kay released Reena and stood. "Not that I doubt your capability, *zintanda*, but the system is complex."

Reena smiled up at her. "I understand. And you really can't get there without the jewel?"

Jasper nodded. "Yes, we are depending on you."

Reena took a deep breath and cupped the jewel in her hands as Bast scurried up to her shoulder. "Let's see if I can do this again."

She shut her eyes and concentrated, the jewel in her hands pulsing in time with her heart. She focused on the base orbiting the planet, its sounds and its shape and its scent.

Almost instantly, blinding light surrounded her, and she felt her father and Auntie Kay grab her as the world inverted and turned upside down. But when the light faded, they were standing in the cold metallic chamber of the Ikroza with the Earth glowing beneath them.

Auntie Kay choked on a sound somewhere between laughter

and a sob before she threw her arms around Reena and pulled her into a crushing embrace, muttering something in a language between Somali and Xhosa while tears streamed down her face.

"Amazing." Jasper stood at the window and gazed down at Earth.

While Auntie Kay and Bast focused on the computer terminal, Reena tucked herself against Jasper's side. They stood together in silence.

"I am sorry, Reena." He kissed the top of her head. "I am."

"I already forgave you, Dad." Reena smiled up at him.

"This was not what I wanted for any of you," he said. "But I convinced myself that Cecelia would be strong enough to do it. I encouraged her to pursue her athletics. I didn't have the same expectations for you."

"I'm glad you didn't." Reena laid her head on his chest. "I hate sports." She pulled back. "And besides, Dad, I don't have to be strong like Cecelia. I can be strong like me."

Jasper smiled at her, his eyes shining as much as Auntie Kay's had. "You are right. And wise. Much wiser than your old dad."

"No, just better looking."

Jasper chuckled and kissed her forehead.

Reena waited for a moment. "Was Eedo Hani really a mighty warrior?"

"She was." Jasper's expression grew sad. "Bold and brave and fierce. She protected the people she loved until the very end."

"She was a hero."

"Yes." Jasper held her tighter. "A hero."

They stood together quietly while Bast and Auntie Kay spoke at the computer.

"Mica was here with me before," Reena said.

Jasper didn't respond.

"Why didn't Auntie Kay want her to come with us?"

Jasper patted her shoulder. "Mica is a good girl and a wonderful friend, Reena. I am glad you have her, and I know you love her." He turned them around to look inside the Ikroza. "But this is bigger than her. It is bigger than Earth, and it's not something she needs to bear."

"She's my best friend, Dad."

He squeezed her shoulder. "I know. And I want you to know that we care about Mica as much as you do. She came from nothing, Sareena. You could have ignored her when you first met her, and you didn't."

Reena nodded.

When Mica had first come to Kansas, adopted by the Sherman family from an impoverished orphanage in Russia, she had been scrawny and malnourished, quiet and sickly. None of the other children had wanted anything to do with her. She'd been skeletal, pale as snow, with hair like a tangled ball of orange yarn.

Reena remembered wondering if all Russian children looked like that.

"We care about Mica," Jasper said again. "But she is just a

girl from Earth. You are a princess of Mercury, Reena."

Reena bit her lip. She didn't really see why it made a difference if Mica was royalty or not. They would be friends regardless, but maybe her father was trying to say something that she just wasn't understanding yet.

Jasper hugged her again. "I am proud of you, Reena."

Reena laughed. "What for?"

"What for?" Jasper looked at her like she grew another head.

"Dad, I didn't do anything." She shook her head. "I put on an armor that did all the work. I rode a dragon who did all the work. I didn't do anything."

Jasper knelt on one knee and took her hands in his.

"Sareena, hear me when I say this." His eyes shone at her. "You were given tools to use, and you used them to defend and protect. That is no less heroic than a warrior who charges into battle with bare hands as his weapons." He tapped the bottom of her chin with his knuckle. "Do you hear me?"

Reena blushed and looked down. "Yeah, Dad, I hear you."

"Little hero, then." He smirked and stood up. "Come. Let us find your Auntie Kay."

They strode arm in arm to the computer terminal where Auntie Kay had been.

"This is dangerous, isn't it?" Reena asked softly.

Jasper's hold on her arm tightened. "Very." His fingers trembled. "There is an ancient evil, Reena, that my sister and the princess guardians of the other planets gave their lives to defeat.

They, along with the great dragon Khanyiso, sacrificed everything to lock this evil away for a time."

"But not forever."

"No." Jasper shook his head. "We do not know how much time we have before she returns, but when she does, we must be ready for her." He tapped the end of her nose. "You must be ready for her."

"Jasper, Sareena!" Auntie Kay's voice echoed in the chamber beside them. "Come here."

Reena ducked out from under Jasper's arm and ran into the chamber with the stone figure of Khanyiso with her wings outstretched. Jasper paused in the doorway to stare, and Reena would have sworn his eyes grew teary again.

"What is it, Auntie Kay?" Reena ran up to her.

Auntie Kay's expression was somber. She stood near one of Khanyiso's great talons, and she pointed to the skin of the dragon's giant knuckle.

"Do you see?" Auntie Kay asked.

Reena narrowed her eyes and blinked in surprise. "Is that—a crack?"

Reena examined the crack in the stone dragon's skin, a gleaming thread of silvery light arcing between two misshapen scales.

Jasper came up behind her and leaned closer to see for himself. "Yes," he said grimly. "A crack in Khanyiso's skin." He cast a worried glance at Auntie Kay. "How long?"

Auntie Kay shrugged. "I have no idea, Jasper." She brushed past them in a flurry. "There is no data. There is no history. Khanyiso may have cracked today, or she may have cracked ten years ago."

Reena ran to catch up with her. "What does that mean?"

Bast bounded along beside them. "Khanyiso sacrificed herself to seal the Dark Queen away. She turned herself to stone, expending the energy to accomplish it. But the seal she used will only remain in place as long as Khanyiso remains stone." Bast scurried up Reena's leg to perch on her shoulders. "And Khanyiso's seal is cracking."

Reena took a shaking breath. "Does that mean the Dark Queen is coming back?"

"Sooner than we expected." Auntie Kay turned back to the computer terminal. "The countdown to her return has begun. She could return at any moment."

Reena paused at the computer terminal, watching the characters on the screen drift up and down. Auntie Kay had switched the computer back to its original language. In the quiet of the moment, Reena could hear the recycled air swishing in the vents.

The pink jeweled Heart of Arawelo burned in her pocket.

"What do we do?" she asked softly.

Jasper came up behind her and set his hands on her shoulders, and Auntie Kay smiled down at her.

"I have been preparing for this day for decades," she said, "seeking out the members of the royal houses who are living on

Earth, gathering them together, working toward the day when I knew we would need to unite." She made a face. "Although I may need to reassess my assumptions of who will actually be chosen as a Dragon."

"How are we going to find all of them?" Reena asked. "Will each one need to get one of the stone eggs in the chamber?"

"Yes. Each egg holds the Khonzi—the dragon partner—of each dragon guardian." Auntie Kay focused on entering code on the computer terminal. "When they are ready, we must locate the next princess."

"What about the egg for Saturn?" Reena asked. "I noticed it was missing."

Auntie Kay smiled to herself. "The Dragon of Saturn is already active, but she is not here. And that is another story for another time, but your powers of observation are impressive, as always, Sareena."

Reena smiled.

"I'll help in any way I can," Reena said.

"I know, little one."

"But I want Mica to help too."

Auntie Kay stopped typing and looked down at her with a raised eyebrow. Reena held her gaze without flinching.

"I think well of your friend, Sareena," Auntie Kay said. "If you believe she can help, then she will be an asset to our cause."

Reena brightened. "She will, Auntie Kay. She'll make a difference. Without her, I couldn't have stopped the *khohlakele* and the *nanto*."

"Very well then." Auntie Kay turned back to the computer. "I hope you are right, Sareena. Our time was short, and now it is shorter still. We know not when the Queen of Darkness shall break free of prison, so we must move as quickly as we can."

"We will." Reena straightened. "We'll win."

"We must." Auntie Kay smiled grimly.

As Jasper and Auntie Kay fell into conversation about some other part of the Ikroza, Reena glanced to the chamber where Khanyiso loomed over the khonzi eggs. As she stared at them, Reena would have sworn she saw one of them crack.

Surely she was imagining that. It was her anxiety getting the better of her.

Either way, whatever time they might have had to get their bearings was gone. The Dark Queen that Auntie Kay feared so much was coming, and if Reena and the other princesses who were yet to be discovered didn't stop her, nobody could.

Reena guided her electric scooter into an empty space outside Towne West Square mall and unstrapped her helmet. The messenger bag she'd fastened to the steering column on the scooter rustled and shifted, and the flap popped open as Bast stuck his pink fuzzy head out.

"Where are we?" He sniffed the air suspiciously.

"Towne West." Reena locked her helmet on the steering bar and secured the scooter to the bike rack.

Bast made a disgusted face at the entryway of the rundown mall. "Why are we here?"

Reena giggled. "Because nobody comes here anymore except old people who need to get their steps in. And it's halfway between Mica's house and my house." Reena held her arm out to Bast, who scurried up to her shoulders and lay down, his tail tickling her back.

"It's safe?" He still didn't look convinced.

"Bast, I promise, anyone here who could notice you isn't going to care." She laughed. "We won't go into the stores, either. Mica and I meet here when we need to talk. There's a boba tea shop inside where we always go, but there are lots of quiet spots where we won't be bothered."

A backfiring muffler made Reena turn toward the parking lot as an antique rust-laden neon green truck sputtered its way toward the entry.

Bast's expression of disgust returned. "What is that creature?"

Reena laughed. "That, my friend, is *Ulilohi*." She pointed to the license plate on the front of the vehicle, bolted in place to a bumper secured primarily with duct tape. The vanity tag proclaimed ULILOHI proudly, and anyone who spoke Cherokee always got a good laugh about it.

"*Handsome*," Reena supplied. "It means *handsome*."

"It is repulsive."

"That's the point."

Bast scoffed. "Humans."

"It's my dad's best friend, Ezekiel." Reena faced the parking lot. "He's dropping Mica off. And I think he probably wants to meet you."

The choking green truck parked in front of the mall entry, but Ezekiel didn't turn the engine off. Most likely because he wouldn't be able to get it started again. His old truck had caused several headaches in the years he'd owned it, but he would never sell it.

The driver's side door swung open, and Ezekiel stepped out, dark eyes smiling at Reena. His boots thwacked on the pavement, and he paused at the curb, still gazing down at both Reena and the pink furry creature on her shoulders.

"Hello, Sareena." His smile deepened. "This must be the infamous Lord Bast." Ezekiel bowed his head. "An honor to finally meet you."

Bast regarded him with a curious sniff but said nothing.

Ezekiel carried a sense of calm and peace with him wherever he went. Reena had always suspected it had something to do with the time he'd spent in the Marines with her dad. Ezekiel didn't speak of that time in his life often, except for the years he was stationed in Japan. It was one of the reasons he'd opened Senjumin, the sushi restaurant. Japanese food was a unique option for a landlocked state like Kansas, but Ezekiel had loved the Japanese culture so much he'd wanted to share it with the city.

Typical Ezekiel. Community first.

The passenger side door of the sputtering truck slammed, and Mica bounded around the tailgate in a bright green shirt, khaki cargo pants, and a floral duster that nearly dragged the ground. Her red hair was trying desperately to escape its French braid.

"Thanks for the ride, Uncle Fox." Mica jumped up on the curb next to Reena and beamed at Bast. "Hi!"

Bast rolled his eyes.

Mica laughed and dug a jar of pickled ginger out of her bag. "I bet you're happy to see me now."

Bast's ears pricked up, and he snatched the jar out of her hands with a squeak. His bushy tail twitched with ill-concealed delight.

"Is that where all my pickled ginger is going, Michaela?" Ezekiel raised an eyebrow at her.

Mica grinned sheepishly. "I marked it down."

Ezekiel sighed. "I will order more." He held out a hand to Reena, which she took. "Your father has filled me in since yesterday." His dark eyes were deep. "Quite a heavy responsibility to fall on your shoulders, little one."

"I can do it." Reena lifted her chin with a smile and glanced at Bast, who was lost in his adoration of the jar of pickled ginger. "Well, we can do it."

"Of this, I have no doubt."

"Dad may not think so." Reena shrugged. "He keeps apologizing for not preparing me better."

Ezekiel stepped closer to her and bent to set a gentle kiss on the top of her head. "Your father fears for your safety, as a good father should, but he does not doubt you, Sareena. He never has."

Reena breathed out slowly. "Thanks, Uncle Fox."

Ezekiel pointed to her and then to Mica. "The two of you stay out of trouble, yes?" He pointed at Mica longer, raising an eyebrow higher.

"What?" Mica held her palms up. "Why are you looking at me like that? I'm not the one who woke up an alien and knocked my best friend off a skyscraper."

"Epic Center is hardly a skyscraper." Reena made a face.

Mica stuck out her lower lip. "Or tried to get me sucked out into space."

"I stopped it."

Ezekiel folded his arms, black eyes sparkling with laughter. "You two have made my point for me." He nodded toward the mall. "Be good."

Reena waved at him as he climbed back into the idling green truck and gunned the engine, belching a cloud of exhaust out its tailpipe.

Mica tucked her arm into Reena's, and they walked together into the mall. Years earlier the mall had been a popular spot for people to congregate, but as the culture of the city changed with the times, the popularity of the malls faded.

And, well, Towne West was practically in the Orchard, and nobody came to the Orchard anymore unless they were looking for a fight.

"So?" Mica nudged Reena with her elbow. "What did you find out? Was Bast right? Are you actually a for-really-real princess?"

Reena nodded. "I am. And Auntie Kay really is too. She's the daughter of the Queen Under the Moon, the one the Dragons of the Diamond Throne are sworn to protect."

Mica beamed. "You're like her bodyguard now?"

"Something like that." Reena led them to the food court at the center of the mall, and they settled in at their favorite table in the corner between two fake jungle-looking plants. Bast sprawled on the table with his jar of pickled ginger and happily ignored them.

As expected, nobody noticed them. The food court workers were all focused on their jobs. The half dozen elderly couples were focused on walking the mall circuit. And other than that? Well, there was no one else there.

Mica bounced over to the ICTea Boba Shop and ordered two large boba drinks, one matcha milk and the other strawberry. Maybe one day one of them would get something different, but they were both creatures of habit.

Reena looked at Bast, still snuggling the jar of ginger.

"Do you want me to open that for you?" Reena smiled.

Bast held it tighter and made a trilling sound.

"Or not." Reena shook her head.

She accepted the pink-colored drink from Mica and shook it with anticipation, watching the little pearls of brown-sugar-soaked tapioca at the bottom shine in the harsh overhead lights.

Mica scooted her chair closer to Reena and propped her elbows up on the table. "So?"

"So."

"You and Kay and your dad went back to the Ikroza," Mica said, sipping on her creamy purple milk tea.

"Yeah." Reena sipped her drink and sat forward. "From what I can tell, Auntie Kay and my dad were some of the only survivors of a war on the Moon. My Eedo Hani survived, but she was hurt very badly. She and Auntie Kay's governess came here, to Earth, to hide because people would be hunting Auntie Kay."

"Since she's like the crown princess, right?"

"Right." Reena glanced at Bast. "Bast is one of eight dragon guardians that are bonded to the princess warriors of the solar system. He was wounded in that last battle badly enough that he had to regenerate."

"Which is why he turned into a stone egg, to heal himself." Mica snapped her fingers.

"And he woke up and hatched when I touched the stone egg." Reena shrugged. "Eedo Hani died when my dad and Auntie Kay were young, and they found a way to survive together and eventually made it here."

"To Kansas?" Mica scrunched up her face.

"Yeah, they didn't explain that very well." Reena chuckled. "There are so many questions to ask. I don't even know where to start with them. But what I know for sure is that the dark power that attacked the Moon was locked away somewhere. That's what caused the giant dragon statue in the Ikroza—Khanyiso. She used all her power to trap that dark force in another dimension, but her power is wearing down. And when she wakes up?"

"The dark power will get loose," Mica whispered.

Reena nodded. "Yes. That means we need to find the other princesses before Khanyiso's seal is broken."

Mica scratched her chin. "Wow. How are we going to do that?"

Reena scooted her chair forward further. "Auntie Kay has been developing contacts over the last few decades, and she has leads on where all the princesses are located."

Mica brightened further. "That's amazing! Where are they? And how can we tell them apart from normal people?"

Reena laughed. "Normal people?"

"You know what I mean."

"Yeah." Reena shook her head. "I did ask Auntie Kay that. She said that all the royal family descendants left on the planets aren't the ones who have the genetic lineage we're looking for, so it has to be the ones who came to Earth."

Mica blinked. "All the planets have people who came to Earth?"

"During the war that brought the collapse of Ebi Inyanga, yes."

"Ebi Inyanga."

"The kingdom ruled by the Queen Under the Moon." Reena looked down at Bast again. "It was a dark time," Auntie Kay said. "But that means there are several generations between the royal families who came to Earth and the princesses we're looking for."

"So, they could look like anyone?"

Reena winced. "They could *be* anyone." And then she smiled. "Maybe even you."

Mica laughed. "Me? I'm not a princess, Reena."

"I didn't think I was either." Reena laughed. "And even Dad and Auntie Kay didn't think I was the *right* princess. You never know."

Mica slurped her drink. "Maybe." She spoke around a mouthful of boba. "I'm just from a lame, hard-to-pronounce orphanage in St. Petersburg."

Reena sat up straight in her chair and saluted stiffly. "*Oktyabrsky.*"

"*Oktyabrsky,* comrade." Mica saluted back.

They both giggled.

Years earlier, they'd started making fun of the name of Mica's orphanage, mostly because it was difficult to say. It had turned into an inside joke between them when they had first been friends.

"But wouldn't it be great if you were a princess too?" Reena spun her drink glass in her hands.

"I'm happy for you to be the princess." Mica held up her drink. "I'll be the princess's best friend."

Reena patted Bast on the head. "I told Auntie Kay that you needed to help us." She smiled. "Well, that you needed to help me."

"Good." Mica sat up. "I was going to help you regardless."

Bast shifted on the table and sat up, his ears twitching. Reena followed his gaze to where a tall black woman approached them.

"Auntie Kay?" Reena turned in her chair.

Auntie Kay nodded as she came to stand at the table. "May I join you?"

Mica stood and grabbed another chair from a different table and brought it for her.

"Thank you, Michaela." Auntie Kay sat down, carefully arranging the folds of her patterned yellow and red dress around her legs. "Ezekiel said this is where I could find you girls." She set a large pouch on the table and patted it absently. "I hope you both are recovered from your ordeal."

She eyed Bast, who had gone back to curling around the jar of pickled ginger.

"We must talk."

Mica glanced at Reena and then back at Auntie Kay. "Do you want me to go?"

"No, Michaela." Auntie Kay set her hand on Mica's shoulder. "I would like for you to stay. Sareena has assured me that your help will be invaluable as we seek to connect with the Daughters of the Stars." She sighed. "And we have less time than I believed before."

"What do you mean?" Reena asked.

Auntie Kay opened the large bag she'd set on the table and withdrew from it a large stone egg, shimmering violet in color. "This is the Khonzi of Haleine. Venus." She turned it and pointed to the obvious cracks beginning to form on the skin of the stone egg. "The dragon within is awakening."

"Yay!" Mica jumped up with her arms in the air. "Another friend!"

Reena grinned at her. "That's great, Auntie Kay. We're ready to help however we can. Just tell us where we need to go, and we'll find the next princess."

Auntie Kay shifted in her chair, suddenly looking a bit uncomfortable. "There is no need to travel, Sareena. The Dragon of Venus is here."

Reena blinked. "Here?"

Mica spun in a wild circle. "In the mall?"

Auntie Kay smiled. "No, not in the mall. But she is in the city."

Reena sat up. "Well, that's even better. Do you know her name?"

Auntie Kay held Reena's gaze. "Yes, Sareena. I know her name. And so do you."

Reena frowned.

Why did Auntie Kay look worried? Reena settled back in her chair, her stomach tightening in anxiety. She already knew the princess? And Reena did too?

"We know her already?" Mica sat down again and scooted forward. "Well, that's handy."

"I assure you, Sareena and Michaela." Auntie Kay looked to each of them. "I am certain of this. The genetic scans are accurate, and the results are definitive."

Mica deflated slowly. "So—you're sure. That's—good. Right?"

Reena sat forward. "Who is it, Auntie Kay?"

Auntie Kay put the egg back into the bag and closed the flap. "The daughter of the royal family of Venus," Auntie Kay said, "is Amanda Beaumont."

Mica's jaw dropped open.

Reena's stomach turned over. "Mandie?" Anxiety and disbelief warred in her voice. "Mandie Beaumont?"

"Yes, Sareena." Auntie Kay nodded.

"Mandie Beaumont?" Mica squeaked. "Miss Perfect-Without-A-Soul? Miss Model-Without-A-Heart? Miss Mean-Faced-Meanie-Without-Morals?" Her voice increased in pitch with every syllable.

Auntie Kay sat back in her chair and tilted her head. "Without doubt."

Mica sagged and flopped on the table face-first. Reena sank back in her chair and rested her face in her hands.

Out of everyone it could have been, of course it would be Mandie.

"She's not hero material," Mica groaned into the table.

Reena sighed. "Well, she's great at throwing bubble tea." She smiled to herself and lifted her eyes to Auntie Kay's face. "Where do we start?"

Author Note

Hello there, amazing reader!

Another day, another book, right? Thank you so much for taking the time to read this one. Reena is very close to my heart personally, and I'm so excited to introduce her and her friends to the world.

I never planned to write for the middle grade ages (between 8 and 12). I had always wanted to write for the "Old Millennials" or the Xennials or whatever my generation is called. You know. The ones who grew up with analog clocks and cassette tapes and Johnny Carson and Saturday morning cartoons. I wanted to recapture the nostalgia and the adventure of those years and repurpose it for people my age now that we're older and life is terrible most of the time (not really but it does feel that way some days).

And many folks from my generation absolutely bought into this vision of fantastic, fun adventure stories from our childhood. I have loved getting to meet so many of you and share stories about what we survived as kids in the 80s. But then that same demographic started giving my books to their kids.

I wrote the books for adults, but I heard that nine year olds were reading them. And loving them. I heard from a particular nine-year-old fan about how much he simply adored Karl Goodson in the Reishosan books.

And that got me thinking: Why not write a series for middle grade?

At this point in my life (I turned 42 this year), most of my friends have children, and a good percentage of those children are in the middle grade age range. Wouldn't it be amazing to write a story for them? Wouldn't it be an awesome thing to write a series that I would have wanted when I was 10 or 11?

And that is where The Dragons of the Diamond Throne takes center stage. This is a series I've been working on for nearly as Lightkeepers and Reishosan. It's the third superhero team that makes up my Heirs of the Mazzaroth Universe. But I had always envisioned it as a story written to the same age group as Lightkeepers and Reishosan—old millennials who missed the storytelling of our childhood.

But who said I couldn't change course and write Dragons for kids instead?

So that's what I did.

Of course it doesn't mean that the Dragons books won't be entertaining for grown-ups. I still love it, and I barely remember being 10 years old. And the industry is teeming with middle grade books that adults love. My hope and prayer is that both kids AND parents love this series as much as I do.

My excitement over this series is multifaceted. Primarily I love the idea of writing books that everyone in the family can enjoy. If you think about it, the lessons we learned from many of the books we Old Millennials grew up with are still valid today and just as necessary—and not just for kids.

But there's something very special about the Dragons series: Diversity.

I started dreaming up the Heirs of the Mazzaroth books when I was nine years old, a goofy little kid growing up in the middle of a Kansas wheat field. So the stories I imagined included characters who looked like the people in my social circle—white, religious Midwesterners. I imagined characters from other places, but—let's be honest—they were all Midwesterners. I didn't know anything else.

But as I got older, my circle expanded. I met people from other places. I made friends with men and women from every race, religion, culture, and climate. I learned to love the surprisingly diverse culture on the street of Wichita, Kansas (seriously, there are so many different people!). And I fell in love with the way that God has made each of us different and beautiful and unique and individual, and it bothered me that my stories were designed to reflect that beauty.

By the time I realized it, though, I was in college. I'd been writing for more than a decade, and I wasn't sure how to pivot. But what I knew for sure was that I needed more connections with people who were different from me, because how could I try to write a story about someone of a different race if I wasn't close to someone of a different race? I couldn't portray someone with a different family culture in an effective way if I didn't venture outside my own home. And if I wanted my stories to make a difference in the lives of people around the country and the world, it wouldn't work if I didn't try to make a difference in the lives of people in my immediate community.

That's where Reena and her family (and the rest of the characters who are yet to be introduced in the Dragons series) came from: a deep desire to tell a story about people from a different culture than my own that still resonates with all readers. Because when you get right down to it, every person in the world is part of the same family. We're all one blood. We may have different backgrounds, but we all need the same things: Faith, Hope, and Love.

I love Reena so much because she's a smart girl. She doesn't do sports. She doesn't do competitions. She's very much an underdog when it comes to physical activity. And that's basically the story of my life.

I have a soft spot for the geek girls, because I am one. And I really wanted to tell a story about the least-likely type of superhero, the one that everybody dismissed and nobody thought could do it, and how it's possible to be Mighty even if you aren't that kind of strong. I wanted to talk about a different kind of strength.

As always, I haven't got the words to say thank you enough for your support and encouragement. Stay tuned for more stories, because this multi-series adventure is just getting started.

Enjoy the adventure, my friend!

Amy

PS: Shout out to my early readers, including the incomparable Makayla Young (she's the one who also makes the adorable plushies of Bast by hand)! Additionally, I want to thank the crew of awesome kids who read this wild story before it released to help me sort through any inconsistencies. **Thank you, everyone!!**

- Audrey
- Gwen
- Erin
- Aria
- Nora
- Cynthia
- Chloe
- Isabella

PS again: And I can't forget to thank my amazing illustrator, Kristen Hildebrand! I told her I wanted Reena chasing a pink red panda in front of the Epic Center … and she did it. She's extraordinary. If you are an author or you know an author who needs some character art or cover illustrations, check her out at
https://instagram.com/artkrisma

Discussion Questions

Since Reena Ellis and the Pink Panda Problem is a book that works for all ages, I thought having some conversation starters and discussion questions might be a nice thing to include.

Who is your favorite character?

Why is that character your favorite?

Would you want to be a superhero? Why or why not?

What was the most exciting part of this story? Why did you choose that part?

What did you think about Mandie Beaumont?

Have you ever had a person pick on you the way that Mandie picks on Reena? How do you handle it?

Would it be more difficult for you to believe that your dad is royalty or that your family comes from another planet?

Explain your answer.

**Why was Reena so sad and upset at the
beginning of the story?**

**Why do you think being a Peregrine agent
means so much to Reena?**

Why does getting to do that thing matter to you so much?

What's something you want to do in your life that you haven't been able to do yet?

**Do you think Reena will ever get to be a
Peregrine agent? Why or why not?**

**Why do you think Reena's dad didn't tell her
about their family's true history?**

If you have a brother or a sister, how does it feel
when it seems like your parents choose them for
something special and not you?

Why is it important for you to understand how
valuable you are to your parents and your
family and the whole world?

Why do you think that Reena and Mica are such good friends?

What sort of adventure do you think they'll get up to in their next book?

About the Author

A.C. Williams is a coffee-drinking, sushi-eating, story-telling nerd who loves cats, country living, and all things Japanese. Author of 20 books, she keeps her fiction readers laughing with wildly imaginative adventures about samurai superheroes, clumsy church secretaries, and goofy malfunctioning androids; her non-fiction readers just laugh at her and the hysterical life experiences she's survived. If that's your cup of tea (or coffee), join the fun at www.amycwilliams.com.

Other Books by A.C. Williams

Check www.amycwilliams.com for where to find them!

The Legend of the Lightkeepers

- Meg Mitchell and the World Between Worlds
- Barb Taylor and the Russian Dolls

REISHOSAN: Samurai Defenders

- Ronnie Akkard and the Brotherhood of Blades
- Stan Hawthorne and the Broken Sword
- Karl Goodson and the Food Truck Fiasco

The Dragons of the Diamond Throne

- Reena Ellis and the Pink Panda Problem

The Misadventures of Trisha Lee (action/romance)

- Finding Fireflies
- Saving Sparrows
- Flipping Fates

Non-Series Books

- A Cowboy for Christmas (sweet romance)
- State Fair Secrets (romantic comedy)

The Heirs of the Mazzaroth Patreon

In case you don't like waiting as much as I do, I've got an option for paid subscribers to read fresh, raw chapters as I write them. I am usually able to get out a new chapter from whatever Mazzaroth book I'm currently working on once a week.

Subscribers also have access to ALL previous chapters of my drafts. Not only that, depending on which tier you support, you can either receive the ebook or the paperback for FREE.

Currently, the chapters available on my Patreon include:

- Meg Mitchell and the Ugly Bird (novella)
- Meg Mitchell and the Unnamed Full-Length Novel (old draft)
- Meg Mitchell and the Still Unnamed Full-Length Novel
- Jenny Mitchell and the Mountain of Fire
- Sam Logan and the Sword of the Sun
- Reena Ellis and the Red Panda Problem (novella)

Chapter-level packages start at $3/month. That gets you access to new chapters as they are written, an ebook for free, and previews of all new character art before it releases.

For more information, check out my Patreon:

https://www.patreon.com/acwilliams_author

The Heirs of the Mazzaroth: Phase 1

KICKSTARTER

The Heirs of the Mazzaroth is an epic story-world where three complete superhero series take place: *The Legend of the Lightkeepers, REISHOSAN: Samurai Defenders*, and *The Dragons of the Diamond Throne*. Since they all happen in the same story world, all the characters share screen time with each other and crossover into each other's individual stories.

This massive adventure series is the result of 30 years of creative planning and dreaming, and while the individual books will be releasing one at a time *eventually* if you want to guarantee yourself a copy (along with a ton of other exclusive features), you're going to want to participate in the upcoming Kickstarter. **The best way to**

get in on all the action is to join author A.C. Williams's email newsletter or to join one of her online communities.

The Kickstarter is designed to allow me to release all seven Phase 1 novels along with all the novellas all at once featuring updated cover art and character illustrations. The books will, of course, be available wide and to the public, but this will be the opportunity to get them immediately when they are available. Otherwise, you'll need to wait for several months in between releases.

Titles (full-length novels and novellas) that will be included in this Phase 1 Kickstarter are as follows:

- Meg Mitchell and the Unnamed Full-Length Novel
    - Barb Taylor and the Russian Dolls (novella)
- Danny Mitchell and the Unnamed Full-Length Novel
    - Stan Hawthorne and the Broken Sword (novella)
- Ronnie Akkard and the Brotherhood of Blades
    - Karl Goodson and the Food Truck Fiasco (novella)
- Jenny Mitchell and the Mountain of Fire
    - Reena Ellis and the Pink Panda Problem (novella)
- Sam Logan and the Sword of the Sun
    - Jim Taylor Novella
- Mickey Mitchell and the Unnamed Full-Length Novel
    - Aoifa MacTiernan Novella
- Ryan Lewis and the Collector of Worlds

I hope you can join me on this exciting adventure of bringing these characters and these worlds to life. I am in the process of setting up a website with more information about how all of the stories fit together.

And in case you're concerned about plans falling apart again (believe me, you're not alone on that score) I am keeping all my Patreon subscribers updated with progress on each full-length novel as it is produced. As of this writing in October 2024, here's where they stand:

BOOK TITLE	CURRENT STATUS
Meg Mitchell and the Unnamed Full-Length Novel (Lightkeepers)	*In Revisions*
Barb Taylor and the Russian Dolls (Lightkeepers)	**Available May 2024**
Danny Mitchell and the Unnamed Full-Length Novel (Lightkeepers)	Drafting Started
Stan Hawthorne and the Broken Sword (Reishosan)	**Available June 2019**
Ronnie Akkard and the Brotherhood of Blades (Reishosan)	**Available March 2020**
Karl Goodson and the Food Truck Fiasco (Reishosan)	**Available September 2022**
Jenny Mitchell and the Mountain of Fire (Lightkeepers)	*In Revisions*

Reena Ellis and the Pink Panda Problem (Dragons)	**Available October 2024**
Sam Logan and the Sword of the Sun (Reishosan)	*In Revisions*
Jim Taylor Unnamed Novella (Lightkeepers)	Concept Stage
Mickey Mitchell and the Unnamed Full-Length Novel (Lightkeepers)	Outlining
Aoifa MacTiernan Unnamed Novella (Lightkeepers)	Concept Stage
Ryan Lewis and the Collector of Worlds (Reishosan/Lightkeepers)	Concept Stage

So while there is a GREAT DEAL of work left to do, I am eagerly anticipating that they should be ready to release on schedule along with some awesome character art and other special edition features.

Keep your ears open and your eyes peeled for updates about all of this. Again, the best place you can get the most recent information is my email newsletter, which is accessible on my website. If you're following me on any of my social media accounts, that's also a good place to start.

I've been building this series since I was nine years old, over 30 years, and what I have learned from the characters and the crazy adventures they've had is wisdom (and fun!) I'm so excited to share with everyone.

Consider this your invitation to come along for the ride! Join my
email list on my website (www.amycwilliams.com) and get updates!